The Land

Robert K. Swisher, Jr.

REAL WEST

FICTION SERIES

Sunstone Press · Santa Fe · New Mexico

DEDICATION

*For Boots, living ghosts, and arrow heads . . . only the coyote
and the crow know for sure . . .*

First Edition

Printed in the United States of America

Library of Congress Cataloging in Publication Data:

Swisher, Robert K., 1947-
    The land.

    I. Title.
PS3569.W574L3   1986   813'.54   86-22966
ISBN: 0-86534-095-1

Published in 1987 by SUNSTONE PRESS
           Post Office Box 2321
           Santa Fe, NM 87504-2321 / USA

CONTENTS

AUTHOR'S NOTE

There is a parcel of land in New Mexico that in our day and age is called a ranch. The man who owns this ranch swears until his dying day his land will never be subdivided into housing lots or ranchettes. On this ranch are ancient Indian ruins, remnants of mankind when the land was not a possession but belonged to all man as his heart and soul. On this ranch are traces of the Spaniards when they came onto the land in search of cities made of gold. Also on the ranch are homes constructed from stacked rocks when the first Mexicans migrated out of Mexico looking for a new life and a new beginning. Around all of these chronicles of time are rusted-out fences when the white man came to subdue the West. This is a story of this particular piece of land and the men and women who have lived upon it. This is the story of love and hope, grief and despair and the Mother Earth. The land is real — the dates and history are real — everything else belongs to the ghosts.

PROLOGUE
THE BANDIT

Manuel Saavedra spurred his tired and sweating horse on. The three mules tethered together and tied to his saddle looked like they would drop from exhaustion at any moment. Manuel for the first time did not care about his animals. There had been too many years, too many lost chances for thoughts such as these. He buried his sharp silver spurs into the sides of the horse once again. "Run, you bastards," he grunted between dust coated lips, "Run for your life and mine."

In his haste Manuel did not watch the land he galloped over but kept his eyes darting from the pointed peak on the horizon back in the direction of the mountains and the Ortiz gold mine. "Another twenty minutes and it will be dark," he hollered to the passing cactus and sharp jagged rocks surrounding him and his sweating animals. "Dark, and we will be safe for awhile."

Once again he dug his spurs into the horse, and once again the animal pulled from deep within himself the power to go on. Manuel stared at the distant peak that was his landmark. Devil's Peak, he thought. Rising like a ghost straight up out of the rolling land.

For miles around the land stretched. Hard clay-based alkaline soil filled with granite and sandstone. Gnarled and twisted cactus rose from between the rocks and salt-corroded dirt. Cactus looking like witches and demons reaching out trying to grab one as they passed. The horse's legs were covered with the sharp painful quills. Manuel's well-worn and dirty chaps were blanketed with hundreds of the tiny daggers.

"Sheepers," Manuel murmured. Sheepers had destroyed the land. The sheep cutting the grass that used to grow between the cactus. Until now the rain would not soak into the earth but only run off in rushing torrents to fill the eroded washes and gulleys.

The sheepers were long gone now. Gone with the Indians and Spaniards before them. Moved to new lands and grasses, destroying as they went. Taking from the land all she would give and moving one. They were peons to Manuel, only peasants, bowing and serving their masters, content to watch their women wear rags and their children walk barefooted over the terrible hard crust of the earth. Content to eat mutton and goat and pray to their Virgin

Mary. Believing in God and hope. Trusting their lives to souls and redemption. They were no better than dogs digging and fighting for the scraps one threw into the garbage.

But not Manuel — he was not a peon. He did not grovel in the garbage or put his trust in communion or gods. There were no gods, no life beyond today or yesterday. There were only memories and hates and dreams of money. Dreams of pretty dresses with many petticoats for his wife. Dreams of shoes for his children and fine horses with saddles inlaid with silver for himself. Dreams of lassos made from the best leather and a carriage he could take his family into town with. He could hear the people speaking: That is Manuel; he is a very rich man.

But now these were no longer dreams. The dreams would become real. He would ride all the way back to Mexico. Back to Mexico and his wife. Back to hold his head high. Back to the dancing eyes of his children with their new clothes. His family would eat beef, not mutton or goat, and he would be free of the world. Free because he was a man, not a peon. He had risked his life and won. After all the years, he had won. In one last desperate move he had escaped the bonds of the poor.

As the sun began to set, Manuel stopped the horse. The three mules with the large bouncing packs skidded to a stop and bumped into the rear of the horse. The horse was too tired to kick but only stood, its nose almost touching the ground, and gasped for air. Manuel jumped from the saddle and in the same motion pulled his rifle out of the scabbard. Letting the reins fall to the ground he stepped away from the exhausted animals and stood gazing behind him into the growing darkness. There was nothing — no telltale dust cloud, no sound of clattering hooves, no cussing of angered men. But he knew they were there. Somewhere in the distance they gathered. Patient, cunning men, checking pistols and rifles, preparing bedrolls and provisions, talking softly to themselves. The manhunters, the enforcers for rich owners of the gold mine. The men who lived off of other men's misery and told tales of dead bandits and outlaws.

Manuel breathed deeply of the cooling evening air. In the distance a pack of coyotes howled. My brothers, he thought, my brothers in life. From childhood Manuel had loved the coyotes. The ones too proud to be tamed. Too proud to beg or borrow. Stealing in with the night to survive. Hiding with the days. They are like me, he thought. They were free, untamed, friends to only their own.

Manuel walked back to his horse and picked up the reins. He slid the rifle back into the scabbard and gently patted the neck of his horse. "My friend," he spoke, "I am sorry for being so rough, but such is life." He took the bridle from the horse's head and uncinched the saddle. Taking a rope he tied one end to the horse's front leg and let the horse go. It would not go far but would spend the night searching for the brittle clumps of grass it could scavenge between the pointed rocks and cactus. Manuel untied the mules and took the heavy packs from their sides. "Follow your friend," he spoke.

The mules stepped gingerly behind the horse and shook, relieved to be free from their heavy loads. Manuel sat down on his saddle and opened one of the packs and gently pulled out a heavy bar of gold. Lighting a match he gazed deep into the luster of it. In his fingers it was like a woman's skin. Soft and warm, the ticket to many pleasures. He had thirty bars, each weighing twenty pounds. Six hundred pounds of gold all stamped ORTIZ GOLD MINE. Manuel looked back into the darkness towards the pinon covered mountain miles behind him. Back to the mountain where the Mexicans like him picked out the precious gold. Picked for nothing but bread crumbs. Day after day, hour after hour until they dropped dead like some lizard or bug. Too tired — too used up to continue.

Manuel placed the bar of gold back into the pack and took from his saddlebags several pieces of jerky, and began to eat. Soon, a few weeks, he would no longer eat jerky. He would be in the arms of his wife, slowly running his hands over her soft warm body. Caressing the dark crescent of her breasts, breathing deep within himself the smell of her thighs. There would be no more lonely nights, no more hard rocks to sleep on — soon it would be over. Manuel lay back on the saddle. "I will sleep and before the sun rises I will be off. Home, Mexico, my little ones and my wife," he thought as the dark engulfed him.

Manuel awoke stiff and tired — the stars, like gold dust above him. He gathered the mules and horse and loaded the heavy packs on the animals. His stomach growled for food but there was no time. He must make it to the Rio Grande. Once to the river he could follow it south to El Paso and then across the border to his home not far away. His horse would need water badly by the end of the day, but even if it was in bad shape, beside the river there would be poor Mexican families who would help him with another horse. Only the white man hated the bandits. But the white man was not poor.

Manuel did not gallop his horse, but walked the animals slowly, trying to watch the ground directly in front of them. The land was filled with gulleys and sinkholes. Traveling in the dark was dangerous but there was nothing else he could do. Around him the cactus loomed in the blackness and in the distance the coyotes howled.

Manuel stopped the horse on the edge of a large ridge that sloped downward and out into an open expanse of land devoid of cactus. At the bottom of the ridge one could see the ancient remains of an Indian pueblo and the four crumbling walls of an old adobe church. Beyond the open plain stood Devil's Peak. The sun was red on the horizon when the earth gave way.

The last sight of the world Manuel and his animals saw was the alkaline soil and rocks of the ridge as the ridge gave way beneath his horse and mules. Laying twisted under the earth, his nostrils filled with dirt, Manuel felt the life leaving his body. "So close, my little ones," he murmured. So very close, were his last thoughts as the land reclaimed a son.

Several hours later it rained, sealing the hard dry soil of the slope tightly over Manuel and his gold.

In Mexico, Manuels's wife stoked the morning fire. The children ran around the front of the small adobe home waiting for the sound of their mother's voice calling them in for beans and tortillas. Manuel's wife walked and stood by the small lone window of the house and looked out upon the dry windswept earth that surrounded the poor house. Her heart was heavy and deep inside her breast she knew she would never see Manuel again. Slowly making the sign of the cross she bowed her head and prayed, Take him, dear God, for the love in my heart, he only did what he had to do.

The six men lost the trail after the rain. They had been in no hurry to chase after the crazy Mexican who robbed the mine. He could only ride out into the dry land and then turn back towards the river. Others had tried to rob the mine. Many had gotten away with the gold for awhile, but they were always caught. Caught and cornered in some dry dusty crevice of the earth. Cornered and shot, their bodies thrown over a saddle and brought back to town for all to see one does not rob the Ortiz mine. But with the rain they had lost the trail, and after two weeks along the river they did not find anyone who had seen the man with the mules.

But the men did not care — it was only a job. A dry hard lifeless job. "Lucky bastard," one man spoke, turning his horse back toward the long ride to the gold mine, "lucky Mexican bastard. Six hundred pounds of gold — his . . . all his."

The wind blew over the earth, moving the fine brown dust over all traces of Manuel. And the earth did not care, or feel, love or hate: it was only the earth, and for the land there is no memory.

But this is not the beginning.

BOOK ONE
THE INDIANS

The first Indians of this land were a community of people. They built their homes from rock and mud in rambling clusters. As families grew, more rooms were added to existing structures. They grew few crops but gathered from the land their food. The men were hunters hunting all animals from small birds and lizards to deer and elk. To them there was a god in everything that was, from the rocks and non-living things to all living creatures. They were a peaceful people not wishing war, but at the same time they were a practical people in that they elected men as warriors. The tribe was the center of life, each person in his own way was different but each was a integral part of the tribe. All worked for the common goal of the tribe. In the summer they wore few clothes, not feeling guilty in their nakedness and in the winter they wore hides and woven garments made from various plants of the region. They were a simple people accepting life as it unfolded around them and a superstitious people, believing in the dreams and visions of their medicine men. They were a people attuned to the earth, not taking more than they could use nor wishing for more than they needed. In their simplicity they were a well-structured society which moved through time with the seasons, accepting the good and the bad as the ways of the world and staying in tune with the earth and land around them.

CHAPTER 1
THE INDIAN - 1575 A.D.

Shining Moon sat beside the small cone-shaped cedar fire and looked closely at the large piece of black obsidian he held in his dark weathered hands. It had indeed been a magical day to find such a stone. He turned the approximately 8-inch stone in his fingers and smiled as the light from the fire danced across its dull black surface. Placing the stone gently on the ground he unrolled a deer hide piece of leather and looked at the tools that were exposed. Here were several hard wood chippers and various assorted pieces of iron ore and deer antler. With these was also a blunted wood hammer. Also in the wrap was a small bow and various rock and wood bits used to drill holes in objects. And in a small leather pouch was a handful of dirt given to him by Sleeping Bear.

One by one he picked up the pieces of hard rock, wood and deer antler and inspected them closely. He did not want to make any mistakes when he began to work on the obsidian. Not one chip would be wrong, not one missed blow with the hammer. Gritting his teeth lightly he chose a well-used antler tine. This would be the one. This antler would take the chips from the obsidian. This antler would form the obsidian into a spear point that would be far greater than any spear point every made by any member of the tribe. It must be perfect — it must shine like the stars and tell all of the love it held within itself.

Shining Moon lay the obsidian on the leather cloth and set the antler tine beside it. He tucked his feet underneath his buttocks and closed his eyes. Slowly with deliberation he removed all thoughts from his mind and in their place formed the picture of his love. He could see Flying Bird walking by a river. Her long black hair ran like the dark murky water of spring down her back and rested on the top of her buttocks. The elk hide dress she wore moved with the grace of her body and he could picture the ripeness of her breasts as they rubbed against the soft leather. In his mind he could see her black piercing eyes and the glitter of the turquoise earrings he had given her in the spring. They had snuck away from the watchful eyes of her mother and gone to the river. Shining Moon had been nervous and afraid to be alone with her. These were feelings he had never felt before. He was a warrior, protector of the tribe, supposed to be brave and strong. He would never forget how his hands trembled as he handed her the small turquoise ear-rings wrapped in the soft hide of a rabbit. What if she did not like them? What if he was rejected? It had taken him many weeks to ap-proach the girl. Many weeks of building his strength, hiding his feelings. Many nights sitting beside his fire staring into the flames, trying to quell the beating of his heart or understand the feeling in his chest when he saw Flying Bird walk around the pueblo. There was no other woman like her. He heard the other men talk of her, laughing and wishing about her. About the other women he too would laugh, but when the men talked of her he felt anger swell up in his heart and a deep burn sweep across his chest. These feelings he hid from the others. But inside himself they lingered.

When Flying Bird had taken the rabbit fur in her small, long, delicate fingers and touched his hand, it had been like lightning sweeping up his arms. And when she giggled with happiness upon seeing the earrings and told him to put them into the holes in her ears, he felt the warm flow of passion sweep through his loins. In all time he would never forget this day. How the wind blew around them. How the river seemed to sing as they stood there. And the look of her back as she ran from him back to the camp unable to understand the feeling that swept over her or the yearning that crept into her upon being with Shining Moon.

As she scampered away he had felt full of life, full of the earth, and he went back to pueblo and taking his best pony he rode out in-to the vast emptiness around the pueblo. He kicked the horse and yelped and hollered to the sun and passing birds. Stopping only when the horse could run no more, he jumped from the frothing animal and stood tall and proud, raising his arms to the sun in praise and thankfulness.

After that Shining Moon would go around the pueblo being careful to be in spots where he could catch glimpses of the girl. Always trying to look preoccupied or busy. But the mother and the grandmother knew. He would catch their scornful glances at times, their eyes burning like daggers into his soul. But he did not know that at night around the fire the old women sat and talked amongst themselves about him, giggling and remembering their youth.

"He is a strong man, that Shining Moon," Grandmother would say, just loud enough so that Flying Bird, grinding corn in the corner, could hear. "I bet his manhood is as long as this stick!" and she would laugh, placing a long piece of wood onto the fire.

Mother would click her tongue and make a sour face. "I suppose he is strong, but I bet Creeping Wolf is much stronger."

To the young Indian girl the comments were beyond understanding. Did her mother and grandmother not see the yearning in her heart for Shining Moon? Were they as unimpressed by her feelings as they had been when she had showed the beautiful earrings? "Not like my husband gave me when I was young and beautiful like you," Grandmother laughed. Her mother had only made a disgusted face.

Flying Bird did not know that the two old women knew her feelings. She did not know that it made them happy and brought back memories of youth and time. She did not know that they had seen Shining Moon follow her into the salt cedar by the river. The two old women were smart and wise with their time. They would let the two meet for brief moments. They would let them see each other from a distance but they would watch and always be close by. The two women loved Flying Bird and a match must be the right one. They knew of her beauty and knew of love, and Flying Bird would not be given to any man on some whimsical feelings. There would be time for the heart to know. Long sad time for the girl they knew but in the wisdom of age they knew it was the best. And no matter what Sleeping Bear, the father, would say, no matter the offer of horses or blankets, Flying Bird would go to the man of her heart. Mother had told Sleeping Bear this and in his love for her he had agreed.

Mother was very thankful for her man, he was a good man, not working her like many of the men did. Flying Bird would have a man like this. But in one respect Mother was concerned over her daughter. Shining Moon was a warrior, destined to be a warrior. Not a medicine man or healer but a man made to protect and kill or be killed. A man who would be gone for long periods of time. But Mother knew time would settle the matter and now she enjoyed talking with Grandmother and watching her daughter squirm in her new feelings of love.

Shining Moon opened his eyes and poked the dying fire with a stick. Placing several small cedar sticks on the embers, he brought the fire back to life. But even the fire was not like the warmth he felt for Flying Bird. Flying Bird was his soul and strength, his waking and sleeping moments. She was in the brightness of the stars and the sweep of wind over a hawk's feathers. She was with him in all things. She was like the land, mother of all creation, strength to him and is people.

Shining Moon once again picked up the rough piece of obsidian. He held the stone up towards the stars and then placed it over his heart and in a muted whisper he prayed. "Stars, dark, moon and earth, give to this stone my heart, make it live with the beating of my heart, make it perfect like the living earth and make it warm to the touch of my woman and my love." He placed the rough obsidian once more in the deer hide and carefully wrapped it up with the tools. It was not time to start chipping. There would be a time but he knew this was not the time. The bundle wrapped and tied with sinew, Shining Moon looked out into the darkness for the shapes of his ponies. Squinting his eyes he could see the shadowed forms of the five horses. He loved Flying Bird even more than his horses and for his horses he would die.

Shining Moon stood and stretched. It had been many weeks since he had been with the tribe. Many weeks since the Old Man had had the dream. Life had been much easier before the old man's dream. Several days before the dream Shining Moon had gathered all his strength and taken six of his best horses and walked through the milling pueblo. He had walked straight and tall to the home of Sleeping Bear and in respect called out to Sleeping Bear. "Sleeping Bear, I bring you truth of my love." Sleeping Bear had been prewarned by his wife in time Shining Moon would come and in keeping with tradition he did not immediately come to the door but stayed inside smiling and poking his old wife. With a smile Mother pushed him towards the door and Shining Moon swallowed trying to find his voice. "I bring you these horses of mine and blankets to go with them for the hand of your daughter." Sleeping Bear scratched his head and pulled tentatively on a large turquoise earring in his left ear lobe. He looked past Shining Moon at the horses. They were fine strong animals, well fed and groomed. Walking past Shining Moon, Sleeping Bear touched each of the animals and then turned. "They do not look like very good horses to me for such a daughter as I have."

Shining Moon did not speak but watched anxiously as Sleeping Bear filled his pipe slowly still eyeing the horses. They were fine horses, too fine for an old man, but he could trade them for many good things. Baskets and blankets for his wife, bear and elk meat for the winter.

Sleeping Bear without speaking went back into his home and returned, his pipe lit with a coal from the fire. He eyed the young man. Such a strong and brave man he was. Standing with his hair greased and parted, two hawk feathers moving slightly in the breeze from his hair. He was naked from the waist up and wore only a leather loin cloth and short moccasins. His muscles were long and lean, taut from many days on his horses. But mostly the old man looked into the young warrior's eyes. It was through the eyes one peered into a man's soul. And in Shining Moon's eyes he saw a sadness, a depth that most men did not have, especially warriors. Warriors were usually rash and wild. They used their women, more content to sit by the fire with other men and tell of their battles and deeds. But in Shining Moon's eyes Sleeping Bear could see deep knowledge, a feeling, the look of a leader — a man not only of action but words. In time maybe a warrior chief, a man of decisions.

Shining Moon watched the old man. Inside himself the world was turning. He felt sweat forming between his shoulder blades and a cold icy feeling creeping into his heart. He must consent. If not he would steal Flying Bird. They would creep from the tribe to live as outcasts if they must. He would take her far away from the people. Far away to another tribe if he had to. She would come. He knew she would come with him.

Inside the hogan Flying Bird could not contain herself. She listened as her mother and grandmother talked around the fire.

"It is of no good," Mother spoke.

"He is only a warrior with lousy horses," Grandmother said. Both women kept themselves so Flying Bird could not get close to the door of the hogan and hear the words of Sleeping Bear.

To Flying Bird it was as though time had stopped. Her heart fluttered in her chest like a tiny frightened bird in a net. Her fingers were like the cold ice of winter and her tongue lay dry and lifeless in her mouth. If Sleeping Bear did not consent to the marriage, she would surely go out into the wilderness around the pueblo and kill herself. There was no life, no reason for being without Shining Moon. Surely she could not live with a broken heart. But try as she may, Mother and Grandmother would not let her get close enough to the door to listen to the conversation of Shining Moon.

By now the word had spread around the tribe that Shining Moon was vying for the heart of Flying Bird, and all the old women and men and children were forming a large circle around the poor anxious warrior. Giggles and laughs circulated throughout the crowd. But they were not mocking sounds. Some people whispered: He will not give her — Sleeping Bear does not like him. Others felt he would without doubt get the hand of Flying Bird. All looked at Shining Moon and saw in him the look of love.

Sleeping Bear knocked the ashes from his pipe and then with eyes glowing he looked at Shining Moon. "I will take these horses, but you must bring me one more."

Shining Moon felt the tensions drain from his body and he cringed at the old man. "I will bring you one more horse in the morning." Sleeping Bear looked at the horses and smiled. He knew he could have asked for five more horses and the young man would have given them.

Shining Moon turned, his heart on fire, and walked through the group, proud and happy. Sleeping Bear entered the hogan and looked at the two women and then at his daughter. And then with a smile he spoke: "You will marry Shining Moon in one month's time."

Flying Bird sank to the ground and began crying. The two women came to her side and cried with her. Women, Sleeping Bear thought, they cry over everything.

As the sun rose the next morning, Shining Moon returned with the horse. He tethered the horse to the pole outside the mud home and sat down.

When Sleeping Bear came out in the morning, he stood. "Come with me, my son," he spoke as they walked towards the bushes. The rest of the pueblo was just waking, dogs barked and fires were rekindled. Standing by a tree, Sleeping Bear began to speak.

"For the next month you may come and see my daughter in the evening. You will sit by our fire and eat with us. You may not touch her or speak to her directly. Any question you have you may ask Mother or Grandmother and they in turn will ask Flying Bird who will answer them and they will answer you. You will not be with her in camp nor sneak with her to the trees. This is my wish, this is my demand. You will at all times treat my daughter with respect and as your equal. She will be the staff in your life and the keeper of your soul." Sleeping Bear turned and looked at the young man and placed his hand on his shoulder. "You will make me proud."

Sleeping Bear began to walk slowly and Shining Moon strode beside him. Around them the earth began to awaken. Birds began to sing and a warm breeze started to blow. Sleeping Bear began to speak once again. "We are nothing but men, my son, who must keep up with our world and learn how to survive. Right now the world is nothing but love to you. There is the song of my daughter in all you see and do. But this will pass as all passes. We are but moments of time. Little pieces of life that are but darting flames. Look around you," and Sleeping Bear spread his arm out and circled the land around him. "This is the true mother, this is the tree, keeper of your soul. A woman is a companion but the land is our life. You must never forget this." And the old man stooped over and took a handful of the dry earth and held it out to Shining Moon. "This is my present to you, this is my wish for you and my daughter. Let your love be tempered by the mother earth. Let your hearts never sorrow for each other and hold always to the truth between yourselves."

Shining Moon held out his hand and took the handful of dirt. He would put it in a pouch and place it with his other medicine things.

Two nights later Shining Moon sat in the home of Sleeping Bear. Flying Bird was in the corner busily cutting deer liver to bake over the fire. Mother and Grandmother walked busily around the room clicking their tongues and feeling warm inside. Sleeping Bear talked on and on of his youth — hunting trips into the mountains. Hard winters. The first coming of the Spanish and how they had driven the Spanish back to the south. But in so doing they had gained the horse. Shining Moon tried to listen but his eyes darted from the face of the old man to the sight of his love who worked trying to quell the beating of her heart with her love so close. The old man was quiet for a moment, Shining Moon spoke.

"Mother, will you ask Flying Bird does she feel well?"

Mother looked at Flying Bird, "Are you well, my daughter? A man in the house wishes to know."

Flying Bird looked at her mother. "Tell the man I am quite well and am to be married soon."

Mother looked at Shining Moon and repeated what her daughter had spoken.

During dinner the women sat quietly in the corner as the men ate in silence. Dinner over and a pipe shared, Shining Moon stood. "I must leave. Thank you for dinner, and, Mother, would you tell Flying Bird there is nothing in life as beautiful as she?" Flying Bird blushed and was silent.

Outside Shining Moon looked at the night sky. All across the heavens was the face of his love. Sleeping with his horses outside the pueblo, Shining Moon could not help but think of his love and their first night to come. He would lay her down softly in the marriage home. With trembling hands he would undo the thongs that held her dress together. He could feel her breasts within his palms and smell the scent of her womanhood as her body desired him. This night he did not sleep well but tossed and turned, dreaming of the charms of his bride and the touch of her skin.

But all of this was before the medicine man's dream. Shining Moon rose early one morning to try and catch a glimpse of Flying Bird going for the morning water. The pueblo was already awake and a nervousness was upon the people. By noon the chief had called all the leaders together and by early afternoon orders had been dispatched. The medicine man had had a dream. A dream that a great tragedy was going to befall the tribe. Over the past years there had been many tragedies. Starting with the Spanish who came and killed the people. They had been repulsed but life had never been the same. This was before Shining Moon was born, but he had been told the stories by the old ones. Since then the tribe had always been wary, always on guard from the strange brown men with their armor and horses.

In the early evening large fires were started and the warriors were painted and dancing. They would go out into the vastness around the tribe and look for danger. Finding danger the brave would ride back to the tribe and tell the chief, Black Bison. Several suns away there was a mountain with a box canyon, the sides too steep to scale by men or animals. Here the tribe would go if necessary upon word of danger and all braves, finding the pueblo empty on their return, would go there. Whatever the medicine man's dream had been, it was a powerful one — one powerful enough to send the men out into the wilderness.

Shining Moon had been heartbroken. So close to his wedding. In the excitment of the day there had been no time to see Flying Bird, and he knew it would be no use to go to her home. Mother and Grandmother would not let him enter. Long after the fires went out Shining Moon sat waiting for the dawn and when he would ride out. He had already prepared his ponies. He would take the remaining five. They were well-trained and the ones he did not ride would follow him. He would change every day. He had been told if within one moon he did not see danger, to return. The chief was wise enough to know dreams were not always what they seemed to be.

Sitting with his horses, for the first time in his life Shining Moon was distraught and confused. He had never felt this way. There had never been confusion in his life. Was love like this — warm and happy, sad and bitter? And if so, why should that be? He sat with the night but could find no warmth in the stars.

Flying Bird lay on her hides and listed to Mother and Grandmother snoring. She stood slowly and crept from the home. She did not know that Mother watched but did not move. Outside the door Flying Bird ran to where she knew Shining Moon slept. She ran, feeling a great sadness in her heart, and as she neared Shining Moon's fire, she could not help but cry out when she saw him. Shining Moon jumped up, hearing her cry, and they circled their arms around each other. They did not speak but each felt the warmth from each other's body and the beating of their hearts merged into one. Stepping back, Flying Bird with a delicate finger traced the outline of Shining Moon's lips. "My husband to be, I fear so for your safety." Shining Moon looked into the dark eyes of his love. "I am forever safe in your love, my little one." Then turning abruptly like a frightened deer Flying Bird ran back to her home and stole back to her bed.

In the morning when Flying Bird went to get water, Shining Moon was gone and she felt empty and alone. Mother and Grandmother in their hearts were sad for her and each prayed to the sun to watch over Shining Moon.

Shining Moon rode, his heart heavy in his chest. Around him the dry southwest air circled over the cactus and rocks. There was no warmth in his soul, no rhythm to his heart. It was as though his heart had been torn out of his chest. There was no happiness with the sunrise, no joy in the circling of the hawks or the squawking of the dark crows. But as the day passed he slowly thought his way out of his sadness. And once again he could see the sky and the birds, "My love, my love,' he spoke to the blue sky, "You go with me in all things."

Sitting back down by the fire, Shining Moon did not rekindle the dying flame. Already to the east the first silver darts of a new day streaked the sky. Five or six suns and he would be back with the tribe. Five or six suns and he would see Flying Bird, and then a few more suns and he would be married. All the weeks he had seen no danger. Nothing but the land, the rocks, the scurrying lizards and small game. The medicine man had been wrong and he was returning to his love.

As the sun cleared the horizon, Shining Moon unwrapped the leather pouch, and taking the antler, he placed the antler on the obsidian and struck the rock. The first chip flew, exposing the deep black luster within the heart of the unworked obsidian. After the first chip, he worked feverishly, striking and moving the striking stone, chipping, feeling, touching the obsidian. Within an hour he had one side of the spear point roughed out. Holding it out to inspect, he was happy and satisfied. He retied the bundle and gathered his horses. Riding, he felt alive and warm knowing the stone was safely tied to his waist.

CHAPTER 2
THE MEDICINE MAN

Man of Darkness held lightly to the shoulder of Lame Deer as she led him outside the tent. It always filled him with joy in the morning to touch the shoulder of his wife as she led him outdoors. He did not know how he would have made it through life without her. Ever since the day when his sight had suddenly left him she had been there. She was his staff and confidante. One who he had hurt deeply years earlier. The knowledge of which would forever pain his heart.

As a boy he was a wild one. Always riding his pony faster and more daring than the others. Unafraid as a young man to sneak in and steal from the camps and settlements of the Spaniards. He was afraid of nothing, always testing his courage. Sleeping with all the young maidens he could. Not wanting love or marriage. Content to sit with the men and tell of his conquests and love affairs. But even as a youth Lame Deer had always loved him. Born with a limp, she was not desired by other men. An outcast by the gods, she was considered weak and inferior. But with all the pain and separation she was of such a heart she did not grow bitter but became inside a woman of great wisdom and feeling. Always ready to help a member of the tribe. Working with the sick or the old. Through her Man of Darkness learned deeply of the heart and the knowledge of sadness.

At times, Man of Darkness would sit and remember when he was young and how Lame Deer would always seem to be close to him. Always within her sight. And how he would ignore her. Afraid to talk with her or be kind to her in fear other members of the tribe would think he was weak. He could remember the day he did marry, how taking his young bride to his tent they had walked by Lame Deer and she was crying. But even with his marriage, Man of Darkness remained wild. It was not long before he was sleeping with other women and spending longer and longer time going into the land to raid the Spaniards. It was after one of his journeys he awoke blind. Going to bed at night he was fine, but in the morning it was as though the gods were cursing him for what he had been and he did not see. He stood and yelled, rubbed his eyes, but there was nothing. Gone was the sight of the world. Within a sun his wife had left him for another man and he was alone.

Soon after, he awoke one morning to the smell of cooking rabbit and he could hear the movement of another in his hogan. Feeling a warm touch on his face, he heard Lame Deer speak. "I have loved you since my eyes first set upon you and from this day forth, I will be your wife in all things." He could hear the slight sobs in Lame Deer's voice. "And in time you, too, will grow to love me," she told him. It was then that his dreams began, dreams that would foretell of the fortune, dreams that came true. And with this, his name was changed to Man of Darkness.

In time the people knew that although he was blind, the gods had done this to him so in his darkness he would be the eyes of the tribe. He would dream and know if the year would be a good year. His dreams told him of good harvests, or good hunts. His dreams had foretold of the coming brown men and also of their explusion from the land. Of impending danger. He was not like other medicine men, sitting for hours in smoky rooms, eating peyote. His dreams came on their own. Cloaked in perpetual darkness, he was one step closer to the other world than other men. And now with his old age, Man of Darkness was the most revered of all the medicine men. No man in the tribe from greatest warrior to the men of the council had as much power over the tribe as Man of Darkness. But now with all the recent bad and confusing dreams, Man of Darkness's heart was filled with despair. Without Lame Deer he knew inside himself he would just as soon be dead and gone from this world.

"It is a sunny and bright day, my husband," Lame Deer spoke as they came out of the mud and rock home. Man of Darkness was still confused and musing over his dream that had sent the young warriors out onto the land looking for impending danger. He stood and breathed deep the morning air and pictured the sights around him. The memories of sight were bright as though he were young. He could see the running children and the dogs. He could see the sunrise and the curling of cedar smoke from the bread ovens. All things he could see as bright and fresh as though his eyes were alive and well and not dark sunken spots without spirit. He sat down on the ground in front of the house as Lame Deer went to the river to fetch water. Taking from a pouch on his belt a soft stone, he began to rub it gently. It was a magical stone, able to drift one into their thoughts, pulling out the doubts and confusions and leaving one rested and secure. But although he had sat the last days rubbing the stone, looking for answers, the stone had not brought him peace or answers but only more confusion and unrest.

Ever since Man of Darkness's gift had been shown to the tribe, he had never felt confused. There had not always been good years, but there had been no confusion, and now he did not know what to do with the confusion or questions. Maybe the gods were taking his powers away. Maybe they were slowly giving his powers to a younger man as yet unknown to the tribe. It was strange. He had tried all his medicines but to no avail.

The dream had come as all the others, unexpected and unsearched. He never knew when the dream would come to him. They just came. Came in brilliant flashes of color and sound. Far more distinct than any mere focus of the eye. There were colors and shapes never seen by man that entered his mind. Shapes and sounds that only he could decipher. But this dream was beyond deciphering. Lame Deer had finished cooking dinner and all around him he could smell the odor of the fresh deer. After eating he had sat smoking his pipe peacefully when the dream came. There had been a large bright red heart that suddenly appeared in the sky. A heart that beat so loud it pained Man of Darkness's ears and made him wince. Flowing out of the heart were the souls of his people. Each soul twisted in agony and each soul was covered with an object from the earth. There were trees and cactus, lizards and birds, deer and elk, buffalo and fish, but they were all dead. Dead and contorted in pain. And then from the heart came the earth. But it was not an earth of mountains and rivers, land and water. It was an earth covered with tall buildings like no man had ever seen. And in the buildings were men dressed in clothes unlike any man had seen. Clothes that fit close to the body and choked one. And the people were sad, but at the same time smiling. But the smiles were short and selfish. With one gasp the earth split open and all the plants and animals upon the face of the earth came out as teardrops. Great rushing torrents of water that were salty and dark. Water that swept out until the earth floated upon it like some floundered fish. And with a great rush the earth began to shrink and the large buildings that stood taller than any mountain began to crumble one upon each other until the earth and the animals and all things upon the face of the earth vanished into a small pinpoint of sand and then the grain of sand disappeared, and there was nothing.

Man of Darkness felt as though a great void had swallowed him. There was no life, no living creature. But then out of the darkness another earth appeared. A smooth orb of darkness that had strange crisscrosses running across it. A taut shiny object stretched between cut trees that crisscrossed the earth and in each of these crisscrosses was a house. Houses like the Spaniards built, but the men and women moving in the houses were not brown like the Spaniards — they were white and black and yellow. And they also were sad. Tears flowed from their eyes but they could not speak. Man of Darkness could see in their eyes great sorrow and unrest, deep fear. Then for a moment the dream had stopped and Man of Darkness took a deep breath, glad the dream was over, but then in another rush of color and sound the dream started again. A great tree with many branches came bursting forth from out of the earth. And on each branch was a member of the tribe. But they were not moving or alive but they were not dead either. And scattered on the tree were all the tools and implements of the people. Unused. And in a booming voice the earth spoke: I am lost. My people are dying. I, the mother, will forsake you, my people.

After the dream, Man of Darkness sat, the sweat dripping off his brow. With his strength regathered, he had Lame Deer lead him to the chief and in clipped statements he told the chief of the dream. But he could not tell him the meaning. There were no buildings taller than mountains, there were no objects that dissected the earth. But there was a danger, and with careful consideration the chief decided to send the young warriors out, keeping behind the majority of the warriors to guard the tribe.

Man of Darkness sat and rubbed the stone, beckoning with all his might for the gods to help him. Around him he could smell the smell of death, but he could also hear the sounds of the children and women. Down from his home several men spoke of the plentiful deer this year and others commented on the abundance of the corn crop. All was well, but there was a cloud, a deep dark impenetrable cloud that surrounded Man of Darkness.

Man of Darkness heard his wife returning with the water. He could tell her walk from the others. The one step and then the sliding of the lame leg. If only he could tell her of the beauty he knew she possessed. If only he could make her heart warm with his love. But whenever he tried to speak, there were no words that could convey his feeling. Lame Deer handed Man of Darkness a gourd full of water. "It is a beautiful day, my husband," she spoke. "Hear the children play. Soon the warriors will be back."

"How is Flying Bird?" he asked.

"Lame Deer smiled, "Her heart yearns more and more each day, but it is a good test of her love. What is love without its portion of pain? Love, as all things, must be tempered with life." Man of Darkness drank the water and smiled. Lame Deer entered the tent to fix the morning meal.

Man of Darkness stood and stretched his tired old body. It had been a good life. All around him he could feel the wonders of the world. He could touch the blueness of the sky and the flight of the birds. He could see the fishes swimming in the river and hear the joy songs of the children. With his feet on the ground and his hands held up to the sky, he began to sing: "Mother, Mother of us all, bring to me the answers. It is dark and your dreams confuse me. I am old and slow, my mind tortures for the truth. Mother, O Mother, Mother of us all, let me taste of the truth. Bring to me the smell of the rain and the taste of the dirt that is our soul. Take from me the darkness that engulfs me not in sight but in mind."

But there came no answers and after a few moments the old medicine man had to sit down and rest. Sitting down on the ground, he ran his fingers over the earth. "The earth has forsaken us," he murmered. "The mother is hiding in her sorrow."

That afternoon as Man of Darkness sat in meditation, the warrior Eagle Claw rode into camp with the news. One day's ride away were over 200 warriors from the south riding towards the pueblo painted and dressed for war. Immediately the chief ordered the pueblo to be deserted and the march to the box canyon one day away to begin. Everything that was not needed would be left behind. Only the animals, weapons and food would be taken. Shelter could be made when they got to the canyon. The chief did not show his fear but deep inside he knew if they did not make the canyon they would perish and the women and young men would be taken as slaves to be traded to other warrior tribes from the south.

Man of Darkness sat and listened to the noise of the tribe as they hurriedly packed important items. But deep inside himself he knew that this danger was not the full extent of his dream. His dream was like the pictures carved on the face of the peak several miles from the camp. The strange peak that rose out of the hills that was an evil place, a place of the ancients. The place where man had been long before his people. Men who left only crude scrapings on the rocks as if to warn others of the peril man walked through with each of his days.

At dawn the tribe moved out. The old were tied to drags behind horses. The women and children carried whatever items they could and circling the mass of dust and animals the warriors rode in full battle dress. The tribe would not stop until they reached the canyon and its safety. But even here the chief knew there would be a great battle and many of his people would be lost. Although the sun rose in all its splendor there was blood on the horizon and a deep sadness in the heart of the chief.

CHAPTER 3
THE SPEAR POINT

Although Shining Moon was anxious to return to the tribe, he would in no way cut short his duties looking for the danger. Instead of riding directly towards the location of the tribe, he cut large zigzags over the land. Never for a moment could he let his love make him deviate from his duty. Although there was not a moment during the day he could not feel the presence of Flying Bird beside him, he knew that his happiness was not the primary function of his life.

Shining Moon rode and looked out across the land around him. At times he felt there were many eyes that watched him.

Eyes of men long dead and gone who had walked this land. In the far distance he could see the pointed peak that forever had been a place avoided by the tribe. But it was strange — even as a child when the older men told him of the peak and its bad medicine, he had always been drawn to the peak. At times when he was young he would stand and look towards the horizon and the peak, and it was as though he was drawn to the strange spiral-shaped formation that loomed up out of the rolling pinon and cedar studded hills. Many times he had walked towards the landmark but the nearer he drew, the more the fear entered into his body, and he would reach a point where he could not continue.

But when he was seventeen years old he had ridden his first pony out away from the tribe and straight for the peak. And this time he was not afraid, and as he drew nearer he felt a great strength overcome him as though the souls of many brave men entered into his body. He was confused at the stories of bad medicine he had heard during his lifetime. Stories of evil spirits that would take the manhood from men and make women lose their voices. Stories of ancient people who would come out with the night and spread disease and hunger upon people who invaded their place of rest.

He rode his pony up to the peak that looked as though a giant hand had reached down from the sky and taken a great handful of dirt and then closed its hand and let the earth trickle through its palm until it was a tall spiral and then with careful balance had picked up a great flat rock and placed it on top. It was a tall spiral with a top like a table. And then with rain and snow and time the sand structure had become rock.

Shining Moon had dismounted from his pony and walked to the rock, and once by the spiral he was amazed by the etchings ground into it. There were round faces that smiled and other faces that frowned. There were marks where men had stood and ground out images of deer and bison and other men. There were large ovals of women's breasts and serpents that spiraled around the rock. Shining Moon had stood and run his fingers over the etchings, and he knew that in time past a man like him had stood here and carved out the faces and images. And he also knew the man was now a part of the earth around him, long dead and turned to dust. His soul a part of the trees and living things that were life.

To Shining Moon, this was not an evil place, but a place of time. A place where man had worked and tried to discover his soul and heart. Here was the mark of men trying to transcend the ages. Men just like him. And then Shining Moon, who had never drawn or thought of drawing, searched around the spiral peak and found a hard-pointed stone, and returning to the peak he spent many hours scratching at the hard rock. When he was finished, he stood back and looked at the horse he had carved on the face of the rock. To him it was not a beautiful horse, but for all time, whoever saw this figure would know it was a horse. And for a moment, Shining Moon felt immortal. He felt beyond the grasp of time and death, love and hate, hope and dreams. He was a part of the timelessness of the rock. His soul would forever stand with the rock. And another man in another age would stand and look at his horse, and he would know that he was not alone. That there was an affinity between men. And Shining Moon was proud, but also a little bewildered. Never again in his life would he feel not needed but would always know he was a part of the chain. A small link that was mankind. From that day forward he was no longer a child, but a man. A man strong and unafraid of the world. But he would never return to the rock. It would never be the same. He would still at times look at the spiral from a distance and be able to retrace the strange faces and images of the ancients and see the horse he had etched upon the stone.

As the sun set, Shining Moon dismounted from his horse. It was still warm but one could feel the touches of fall approaching. Shining Moon gathered enough wood for the evening and then started the fire. The fire flaming, he took out the spear point. Over the past five days the rough obsidian had now become a 6-inch point, the first cuts being taken to form the center line sloping to each side and the point. Now he could take small chips bringing the edge of the point to razor sharpness. With each day the point became more and more a thing of wonder. Even to Shining Moon, he did not understand how he could have created such a beautiful point, although he knew it was love that guided his hand.

When at times during the day he would stop his pony, he would take from his pouch the point and hold it up to the sun. With the sun rays the point seemed to come alive and dance in his fingers. He could see the flowing dress and hair of his love. Inside the point he could feel the beat of her heart and the warmth of her breast, naked against his chest. Inside the point lay the seed to their children and the desires of his passion. And always after he put the point back into his pouch, he did not yearn for Flying Bird but felt her around him, her eyes guiding him and watching over him in all things that he did.

Shining Moon looked closely at the point and smiled, and then he took it and began chipping carefully on the edge. Soon in a few days it would be finished, and then he would take his drill and drill a hole though the end of the point. Through this hole he could put a thong, and Flying Bird could hang the point from her waist. Around him the night grew dark and the stars emerged bright and shiny and timeless. And for Shining Moon there was no time, no darkness, just the earth and the night and the feeling of warmth that came upon is heart.

In the morning Shining Moon once again mounted his pony and started his zigzag pattern back towards the people. It was a glorious day. On the horizon two hawks rode the updrafts for hours, looking for the scurrying rabbits or ground squirrels, and all around Shining Moon was peace and contentment.

CHAPTER 4
THE FLEETING

After a full day's traveling, the Chief Black Bison knew his people were tired, but he also knew they dare not stop. The enemy would have found the abandoned pueblo by now and would drive their ponies on trying to catch up with the slow moving people. Black Bison was a good man and had been a good leader.

But after many years, Black Bison was growing tired. There had been so many things he had missed in his life. There was never time to sit and enjoy his children or his wife. His life must be the people. There was always some dispute or danger, some decision, filling his mind. If it was not the medicine men with their dreams and incantations, it was some man wanting another man's wife. If it was not passion or hate it was the weather or a bad harvest. It seemed there was always something. It was a curse to be the leader. A curse to have to make the decisions.

Over the past several years Black Bison had wanted deep in his heart to take his wife and ride out into the wilderness. Out, away from the people, and build himself a small home. A home he would never have to leave. A home on some mesa top where he could stand during the day and look out upon the earth in peace. There had truly never been peace in his life.

When he was a young boy, the Spaniards had come into the land. A cold, greedy people. A people who did not understand the people or their ways. A people who only wanted to take from the earth and never return anything. Life for them was to conquer and die. To die so they could go to some heaven in the sky. Life to Black Bison was to live to see the sun and smell the rain, to make love to his wife and play with his children. But there had been so many battles. So many raids on the Spanish, so much hatred and revenge and so much fear until the Spaniards were driven from the land.

Whenever it seemed there would be peace once again, there would be danger. Not danger from the Spaniards but danger from the southern Indians. Indians unlike his people — these were cold-hearted marauding people, people who took what they needed from weaker peoples. Man was such a strange creature. Unable to live and let live. Always desiring, always hating, always wanting. It seemed there was no end. It was almost a shame to bring people into the world now. It was not like his grandfather told him the world used to be like. It was not a good place.

Black Bison looked from his pony at the procession of his people. There were ninety women, thirty-two children, twenty-nine old people, and over 100 warriors. Out still scouting were over twenty other warriors. Looking at his people plodding through the dry crust of the earth, Black Bison could not help but feel what would another man want with these people? Cannot we just live in peace with the earth?

Black Bison knew the people wanted to rest. He knew the horses were tired and hungry, but they must push on. Soon they would be in the canyon and the people could rest while the warriors took shifts watching and preparing for the battle. They would build fortifications across the mouth of the canyon and hope the gods were with them. He knew even the women would have to fight and the young boys. They were no match against the 200 warriors in the open, but cornered they would fight, fight to the death every man, woman and child if necessary before they would be slaves to any man.

Black Bison's father had been a great chief. A good chief. And when Black Bison was young, his father had never bothered him with what would be his destiny. He was shown no special treatment or care, but was allowed to play with the other boys of the tribe. It was only when he was twelve years old his father took him outside one day to the top of the gently sloping ridge above the tribe and pointing, he spoke.

"All you see will be yours. The heart and souls of all the men and women and children will weigh on your back. For them you must live and breathe. From the day that I die you will never be able to love only one woman, for you must love them all. All children will be yours. The future of our people will be your decision and your decisions will become great burdens on your heart."

And from this day forward, Black Bison was taken from the other boys and kept with his father at all times. He sat in council meetings, he listened to the medicine men. He listened to his father make decisions, and he grew to learn the respect and power his father held, and he knew that one day it would also be his. But he also began to feel the segregation from the other people of the tribe. He was different. He was to be chief.

While Black Bison rode in his thoughts, six braves who had found each other in their search for danger caught up with the tribe. They had ridden around the invaders. It would be very close to see if the people would make the canyon. Black Bison chose fifteen warriors who would remain behind and try to slow up the enemy, hoping it would give the tribe just enough time to make the canyon. Each of the young men knew he would die, and Black Bison looking at them could not but feel a great sadness in his heart. They were so very young, so full of life and joy. Looking into their faces he saw strength and pride, and he thought to himself how many children would these brave men have brought into the world. How many great things could they have done. It was such a waste, such a deep sorrow. As the tribe moved on, the women began a low deep wail, knowing that blood from the people would spill onto the earth. And the wail would not stop until the tribe reached the box canyon.

As the tribe disappeared from the sight of the fifteen, one of the warriors began to dance and yelp a song: "I who am chosen to die, will die with the blood of many enemies." Soon the others were dancing and each in his words and thoughts made peace with the world and prepared to face the enemy and die brave and proud.

Several hours later, when the 200 warriors from the south approached the fifteen, the chief of the invaders, Blue Sky, was astonished. The fifteen sat upon their horses, painted for war.

33

From their hair strung feathers and from their ponies' manes were scalps of other enemies. The chief raised his lance and stopped his men. The fifteen were a beautiful sight, a sight of defiance and life, a sign of strength, and he could not help but feel respect for the men. He motioned to his men and asked in a loud voice, "What fifteen do I have who will engage the brave ones?"

Immediately fifteen warriors broke from the pack, their ponies prancing and fidgeting. Blue Sky lowered his hand and the fifteen kicked their horses and tore at the men.

Black Bison's fifteen warriors in unison began their war cry. The fighting was furious and bloody. Men ripped into each other from frothing, kicking horses. Knives tore into flesh and stained the earth, and when it was done, eight of Black Bison's men still stood, while around them lay fifteen of the enemy and seven of their own.

The chief once again raised his hand and eight fresh braves pranced forward. "Kill the brave ones," he commanded, and the eight tore into the eight tired Black Bison's men. But once again when the fighting was done, four of Black Bison's men stood while all the others lay dead.

With this the chief sent out onto the bloody field a man under a banner of truce followed by several men with food. Dropping the food on the ground the man spoke to the bloody survivors. "Eat and sing your death song, brave ones, for in the morning you die." With this the band of invaders spread out in a large circle around the four men and dismounted.

That night, surrounded by the campfires of their enemies, the men sat in a circle and ate, and then, throughout the starlit night, they sang their songs and relived their lives.

At times one would stand and shout into the darkness, "I am Snake Man, I am not afraid to die. You are but women in our way." And the warriors circling the four could not but be impressed by their enemy. Inside the hearts of the four men, they knew they had won, for with each passing minute the tribe grew closer and closer to its destination — the safety of the canyon.

With the dawn, the invaders mounted their ponies and the four braves faced in four directions (north, south, east and west) and watched as the circle around them grew tighter and tighter, until by sheer numbers they were beaten from their horses and trampled into the ground by the hooves of the horses.

In ages to come there would be no trace of this battle. No

monument to the courage of the men, no eternal flame to spur on the imaginations of the young. There would only be the rock and the cactus. The cedar and pinon trees and the lonely howl of the wind, forever shifting the dirt.

CHAPTER 5
SANCTUARY

By sunrise the next day the tribe arrived at the box canyon tired and exhausted. The canyon was cut out of a large granite hill. Too steep on the sides to be scaled by men or animal, its entrance a small opening no more than 100 yards across. The canyon itself in depth was no more than 50 yards. In the opening were large boulders scattered and crisscrossed across the mouth, making any entrance difficult. Between these boulders were ancient twisted and gnarled cedar trees, providing even more protection for the tribe. At the rear of the canyon was a small spring that bubbled and filled a rock hole about 5 feet across.

Even in their exhaustion the women were put to work gathering firewood for cooking fires. All dead wood was dragged into large piles. Next warriors, by hand and with horses, piled rocks between the already protruding boulders to form larger defenses. Then small shelters were erected anywhere they could stand. Crude shelters from wood and stone. Then and only then did the women and children sleep and the warriors gather for council.

The warriors were divided into three groups. One group would be to the front, behind the boulders. Another with bows would scale the sides of the canyon and rain arrows down upon the enemy and the other would stay behind the front defense, filling in men as others fell from wounds. Several men were sent out as sentries to return when the invading warriors were sighted.

With the darkness, the camp became silent. Women and children slept in the crude shelters. Warriors took turns sleeping. Overhead the night was bright with the full moon. Black Bison walked amongst his people, heavy of heart and deep in meditation. Man of Darkness had not had a dream. The spirits were not talking to him. This battle would be up to man alone.

In the morning Black Bison sat on a small rise within the canyon and looked at his people. He was very proud of his people and filled with emotion. Below him old women, bent and twisted with time, carried heavy loads of wood and piled it on the growing stacks. Old men sat working arrow shafts, their fingers barely able to withstand the pain. The children worked with the others but too young to know of the danger around them, they laughed and sang as if it was nothing but a great adventure that would end soon and they would go back to the pueblo.

Outside of the canyon men searched quickly for game, hoping and praying they could kill enough to feed the tribe during the up-coming battle. Around the rocks and trees of the canyon, birds darted and fluttered, chasing bugs. Overhead the sky was blue and small powder puff clouds moved lazily, as though dancing with the changing seasons. It was a good day to go out onto the land with one's love and make love beside a river. Letting the cool air touch one's skin.

Black Bison stood and looked out beyond the canyon and spoke to the breeze and the sky and his unseen enemy. "Whence do you come, my enemy? What have I done to bring you from the south with your pain and destruction? We are a peace-loving people, content to grow our corn, content to let children sing and play. Happy to let our warriors grow to old men without the taste of battle. But now you come, come like some dark demon with the day, bringing to our hearts sorrow and pain. Bringing to the lives of our women fear and grief. The sky is blue, but the earth will be red with our blood. And now we, with our love of peace and the mother earth, will fight you to the end. You will not make us captives to your bidding. We will not lay down before you like whipped dogs." And with great sadness Black Bison lowered his head. "But I pray, mother of us all, in our battle do not make us hate. Life is too short for us to hate."

Black Bison walked down into the canyon. He must go see Man of Darkness. Maybe he had had a vision. Maybe the gods had spoken and they would help Black Bison and his people.

CHAPTER 6
FLYING BIRD

When Flying Bird rose and went to get water the morning Shining Moon had ridden out looking for danger she did not know if she could withstand the pain of separation. Mother watched her daughter closely for several days, and then one afternoon she took Flying Bird aside and shook her firmly and spoke.

"You are to be married now, my little one, it is time to be a woman, not a child. There is much pain in this life but we must be strong."

After this, Flying Bird held her tears, and although her heart was breaking she helped her mother and grandmother and kept her mind busy by working all her waking hours. When the brave returned with news of the invaders, she could no longer feel pain but was caught up in the frenzy of breaking down the pueblo. People rushed everywhere and many good and wonderful things were left behind. Pots that Mother and Grandmother had worked laboriously on were broken to release the spirit of the maker from them. Dried corn and beans were poured into large baskets and tied to litters behind pawing and snorting horses growing excited by the milling, chattering people around them. With the excitment and growing fear, Flying Bird felt growing in her stomach tight knots thinking about what the invaders might do.

She herself had never seen or been close to a battle. But she had heard tales of what strange men did to women of other tribes. Women would be tied to the ground and men at will would penetrate their separated legs. There were even tales of after the women were close to death, they would be cut up and fed to the dogs of the invaders.

When finally the packing was done and the tribe formed into a jagged line, then and only then did Flying Bird once again think about her love. Why me? she thought — so close to our wedding date. Surely the gods smile on us, there is no love like ours, no love ever in the world. And as they marched circled by the warriors, Flying Bird could not wail like the other women. Her sadness was beyond pain or sorrow but was a dark emptiness that seemed to sap all the hope from her body. My love is gone, she thought to herself. Gone out into the wilderness. Gone to find the danger that follows now at our heels like some evil wolf following a wounded deer.

With the beginning of the march Flying Bird was oblivious to the sound and movement around her. She walked in desolation. One step in front of the other, hour after hour after hour. She did not feel the weariness creep into her feet and then up her legs. She did not feel the blisters slowly forming on her heels or the weight of the straps from the basket she carried filled with beans. She only felt the heaviness in her thoughts, and thought terrible thoughts about Shining Moon. Deep inside herself she knew she would never see him again.

Mother walked slowly behind her daughter. And although she was tired she carefully watched Flying Bird. Inside herself she knew how the little one ached. But what was one to do over heartbreak? There were no words or helping things. There was nothing but the deep bitterness of it. The sleepless hours and the shallow days. Silently in between her own sorrow, she prayed for Flying Bird, hoping she would find strength and grow strong. She would watch the young girl who every other minute or so would reach up to her ears and touch the turquoise earrings Shining Moon had given her. "He is with you, my child," Mother spoke to herself, "in all things he is with you. Now you see the bitterness of love, the longing and heartache. The first feeling of separation. Now you see you must learn to accept. Love is all things in happiness and agony." Mother made a sour face and spit on the ground. Men, she thought, Love . . . and she let her thoughts trail off into happy thoughts of the past.

She remembered when she was a small girl and how she had longed for a brave named Tall Tree. He was such a handsome, brave young man, so full of life and health. When they were children she had fallen in love with Tall Tree, and as she grew up she would dream of the day he would ask her to marry him. But even as a youth she knew Tall Tree would never desire her. She was far too plain and not beautiful like other girls, and Tall Tree was so handsome he would never marry a girl like her. But still she held onto her dreams of him. Watching as they grew together, he becoming more and more handsome and she staying plain and in her heart ugly.

It was a cold winter day and she was fifteen years old when the news came. Tall Tree had fallen through the ice of a river far to the north and was never found. Mother had felt as though the same cold river water flooded over her heart. For many suns it seemed she could not sleep, and in all her waking moments the cold of the ice held a tight hand around her heart. But in the spring Sleeping Bear had asked for her hand and her father had taken three good horses for her.

At first when the match was made, Mother hated Sleeping Bear. He was not handsome like Tall Tree. He was a short little man, not a warrior but a grower. A man who worked in the dirt. He was not brave. She told herself she would run away, but she knew in her heart she would never do that.

The day of the marriage she was sad, but Sleeping Bear sat across from her on the elk robes and looked deep within her eyes. For the first time she saw a great gentleness in this man of the earth. After several long moments, Sleeping Bear spoke in a soft deep voice. "I know that your heart rests with the spirit of another and I know I am not the most handsome man of the tribe, but I promise you in all things of my life you will be by my side and in all things I will treat you with truth."

That night Sleeping Bear did not come to his new wife, but they sat and talked about many things. And in the morning as the sun rose, Mother stood with deep feeling in her heart and she took off her wedding dress and spoke, "Come, my husband, and lay with me with the rising sun."

And Sleeping Bear entered into his wife with a gentleness of the earth and a touch that was soft and pleasurable. And never again did Mother compare Tall Tree with her husband nor wish for another life. Life had been good with this man whom she loved deeply.

After a day of traveling, Flying Bird was oblivious to the movement around her. Thoughts invaded her mind like bolts of flashing lightning that she could not control. Shining Moon's face would appear before her, smiling and laughing and then in the next flash his face would be contorted in pain and blood would be running from a large gash in his side. But there was one vision that kept returning to her tired mind. Shining Moon was sitting by a small fire. All around him was black, but in his hands was a large glistening spear point. It was a spear point like none Flying Bird had ever seen. It shone like the stars and seemed to pulse with life and being. She could see the concentration as Shining Moon struck the chips from the living stone and feel the beat of her love's heart and the sound of his breathing as he worked.

When the tribe reached the box canyon, Flying Bird was not conscious of thought or movement around her. Her body was racked by unfelt pain and her heart was only a dry stone in her chest. There was nothing, no air filtering into the lungs, no fleeting creatures before them, only darkness. She did not remember gathering wood or helping Mother and Grandmother build a small shelter. She did not remember the cool air of night nor laying down on the ground outside the shelter. She did not remember anything until the dawn when she awoke at first not knowing where she was or who she was with. Looking at the rising sun, the memories slowly came to her and with the memories the deep feelings of longing were released by the sun's rays on the rocks of the canyon and by the small darting birds that greeted the day.

And with this she realized Shining Moon was in all things. He was in the earth and the trees. The sky and the heavens. He was within her, held tight by her spirit and her caring. He was in Mother and Grandmother and Sleeping Bear. There was nothing in the world he was not a part of and she knew he would always be a part of her in all things she did during her life. And in that moment, that small period of time, Flying Bird was no longer a child, but a woman.

Grandmother was the first to notice the change. It was deep in Flying Bird's eyes. A depth of vision that youth does not have, a vision of time and death. A battle fought in the mind that settles deep within the eyes of men and women. Seeing this, Grandmother walked over to Flying Bird and took her in her arms and held her close to her large sagging bosom. "My child, my child," she spoke deeply, "now there is only the future."

During the day while the scouts went out looking for the invaders, the women escorted by braves went out and brought in more wood. They gathered the green pinon nuts and setting snares caught as many chipmunks, rock squirrels and rabbits as they could. Although the canyon was hard to attack, it was also impossible to escape from. There was only one way out and that was the way they had entered. They must have wood and food. Black Bison set up cooking stations and split the food into rations. There would be no full stomachs now, there would only be enough to keep one alive. The warriors would receive the larger rations. Already the older horses had been killed. Their flesh cut from their bodies in long strips drying on the rocks in the sun. Burros and young horses would be next.

Late in the afternoon the scouts returned. One thousand yards to the front the invaders had stopped. The standoff would begin. That night the tribe heard the songs and drums of the invaders. All night the chants went on until with the dawn the warriors, guarding the front of the canyon, looked out and saw the invaders on their horses. A man with nothing but a loin cloth and a lance kicked his horse forward and rode, his back straight and true, towards the canyon. Stopping only feet from the first warriors, he threw the lance into the ground and with motions of his arms and hands, told how his chief, Blue Sky, wished to speak with their chief. The message delivered, Black Bison several minutes later rode out of the canyon. Not a sound emerged from the lips of the people as he rode past. Not a look of fear crossed his face, not a sign of sadness. He was like a stone, untouchable, brave, true and hard.

Blue Sky watched the chief ride out of the canyon and dismount and sit on a large boulder. Blue Sky felt a deep respect for the man. His fifteen warriors had indeed been brave men. Surely now their spirits were in the heavens. They were true men, true fighters, and to Blue Sky there was nothing but war and death, strength and boldness. His people were far different than the people of the north. He had been told by his scouts that these people were mere farmers. That they would surrender like women. He had been told that their braves were weak like dogs. But he knew this now not to be true. His own people were hunters and invaders. They took from the weak of the earth. They were the chosen ones. Made and created to trample other people of the land. Blue Sky was not an evil man but he was like all men of conquest obsessed with their dominance, feeling they were the only people of the light. Not wishing or caring to feel the kinship of mankind. There was nothing but kill or be killed, conquer or forever live in shame. And this small tribe of women and children and old men with its small band of warriors would die as sure as their chief sat on the boulder waiting for him.

Blue Sky dropped his lance to the ground and rode out away from his braves. It was a beautiful day. One could feel the touch of the cool season and he felt invigorated and brave. He knew that the eyes of his warriors rode with him. He knew all of them wished to be like him. And in this feeling of power he found great strength. Approaching Black Bison he slid easily from his horse and walked up to the man. Black Bison stood and Blue Sky immediately saw a man of stature and strength. This chief was obviously not a mere grower of corn. Blue Sky made the motion of friendship and Black

Bison responded. Dropping to the ground and sitting, Blue Sky took from his belt a long pipe and lit the tobacco with a coal wrapped in a reed-lined leather pouch. Puffing deeply on the pipe he passed it to Black Bison who in turn breathed deeply the strong white smoke.

"Destiny has brought us to this place," Blue Sky spoke in sign language. "It would be far easier to surrender your people to me. So many of our people will die."

Black Bison sat and did not reply, but looked directly into the chief's eyes. After several moments, Blue Sky stood. "There is no reason to talk. Go back to your people and prepare to die."

Black Bison was no sooner back into the mouth of the canyon when over one hundred warriors of Blue Sky's yelled and charged their ponies into the rocks. But as they entered the mouth of the canyon, sheets of arrows fell upon them from the sides of the canyon and as soon as it started the first battle was over. Twenty-five of Blue Sky's braves lay dead or wounded and not one of Black Bison's. The wounded were soon dead, as warriors stole out from the rocks swiftly cutting their throats and taking from their bodies weapons and other useful items; also gathering the spent arrows.

Blue Sky, watching the quick skirmish, felt a deep anger spreading through his body. He had fallen into a trap. The fifteen braves were left behind to do exactly what they had done. Slow him and his braves up. He should have just trampled them into the ground with his entire force of men. But he had not, and now this battle would not be easy. His men were not prepared for a long battle. They did not have great stores of food, but were prepared for quick moving attacks, depending on their wins to gather food and restock arrows and weapons. He had made a mistake and now he must sit with his under-chiefs to decide on a course of action. When the survivors of the attack returned, he had the men all dismount and set a more permanent camp. In the morning they would resume the fight.

The people of the tribe were overjoyed with the first battle. They had not lost one man and maybe the gods were with them. Maybe the invaders would see the difficulty of the situation and go as they came. Disappearing forever into the land. But when Black Bison consulted with Man of Darkness, the old medicine man was still without dreams or visions, and Black Bison knew there would be much suffering and death before the ordeal was over.

CHAPTER 7
SHINING MOON RETURNS

Shining Moon lay the drill down on the ground and picked up the spear point. The hole was clean and exactly where he wanted it. Forever men would know he, Shining Moon, had created this point as they marveled at it hanging from the waist of his wife. With the completion of the point, Shining Moon felt a peace settle over him. He took the point and held it in both hands and raised it towards the sun. Blues and greens, reds and purples escaped from its black insides. It captured the golden ray of the sun and transformed them into all colors of the earth. It was like sunset and sundown. Placing the point on the deer hide cloth, he took the chipper and hammer and the drill and dug out a small hole in the ground. These would return to the earth. Never again could he use them. Their magic and power had been extinguished in his work. Shining Moon stood and gathered his horses. He would ride to the tribe now. He had found no danger. His duty was completed and he could return to his love and his marriage.

Riding he thought of his wedding day. Flying Bird would be dressed in her finest dress. Beads of red and blue, green and white would flow over the soft deer skin. From her hair would be small feathers from song birds and around her ankles delicate bells that would ring when she walked. Shining Moon would wear long elk hide britches with bead work down each side of the leg. His shirt would be laced with hawk feathers and his hair would be greased and parted in the middle. Around his waist he would wear a beaded belt. The beads depicted strength and love.

Fore the entire day before the ceremony he would be segregated from the tribe as Flying Bird would be segregated. The women would build a tent for them out past the others, and in this tent they would place many elk and buffalo hides, making a soft and deep cushion for the lovers. Inside there would be food for several days. Dried venison, dried fish, corn and beans and several gourds of water. Riding, Shining Moon could hear the women singing and see the sly glances of the older men, remembering their wedding night and the soft curves of their young wives. Of course there would be pranksters. Young boys sneaking up to the tent late at night. Pelting the tent with stones to disturb the lovers. And of course Shining Moon would have to run outside, feigning anger, yelling threats to the retreating boys.

After the lovers were married, Flying Bird would be stolen by his friends, and only after much bickering and bartering would he be be able to buy back his bride. Shining Moon rode and his heart was as the light spring breeze, as happy as a song bird greeting the day. There was no danger, there was nothing but his thoughts and his love.

Late in the afternoon, Shining Moon rode up to the edge of the sloping ridge that overlooked the pueblo. But when he stopped and looked down, his heart was seized by a terrible empty feeling. Below was nothing but signs of havoc. Scattered everywhere, pots and other articles of the tribe. He kicked his horse and rode recklessly down the face of the bluff, riding into the desolate village. He jumped from his horse, his heart racing, and ran around, looking at the desolation. There was no sign of battle, no blood, no dead animals. But he knew one of the braves must have discovered the danger, and the tribe moved quickly towards the box canyon.

Shining Moon walked quickly to Flying Bird's hogan. Sitting outside, a great anger arose in his chest, and he turned his face towards the sky and a deep grief-filled yell came from his throat. "Those who have caused this will die. I will tear their hearts from their bodies and lay them out for the buzzards to eat." Shining Moon walked back to his horses and mounted one. Following the tracks of his people, he began to follow the fleeting.

As night approached he came across the hoof prints of many horses, and he knew now what had been the danger. By the tracks he figured the tribe had been gone almost ten suns and the invaders were no more than one sun behind them. Shining Moon did not stop but continued to ride and change ponies randomly. By dawn he was tired, but he would not halt. Burning deep within him was the sight of his people and the sight of his love forced to leave their homes and run and hide like some mad and wild beast. By nightfall he stopped and rested, but again he did not sleep. His heart raced in his chest and his mind grew hard with the thoughts of death to his enemies.

Two days later Shining Moon, hiding with the dark behind a large cedar tree, saw the invaders' fires. Directly to their front he knew the box canyon lay and inside his people. Somewhere with the rocks was Flying Bird. So close, but so very far away. He wanted to take his pony and ride through the enemy and into the canyon, but he knew this was a foolish act. Instead he rode back away from the enemy to sit and meditate on his actions.

Stopping about a mile from the invaders, Shining Moon tied his ponies. He took from his horse his bow and quiver of arrows and made sure his knife was secure on his belt. He felt for the spear point, wrapped in his pouch. Walking away from the horses, he sat down, and taking deep breaths, closed his eyes. He did not think of Flying Bird but only of the invaders. And in time he decided on a course of action. He would not break through to his people, but would instead with each night sneak in with the enemy and kill as many as he could. Silently, like a snake, he would creep close to them and cut their throats.

The next morning Blue Sky once again sent his men charging into the mouth of the canyon and once again they were repulsed. But he knew now the braves protecting the canyon were also losing men, and he also knew soon the men on the sides of the canyon would run out of arrows. It was only a matter of time. Blue Sky had lost thirty-five warriors. Far more than he expected. During the day the bodies left on the ground were covered with crows and vultures, and those killed earlier were beginning to bloat and stink.

But to Blue Sky this was nothing. They were men born to battle — born to die on some piece of earth in some strange land. Born to be eaten by the coyotes and buzzards. It was the way, the only way for men such as he. Blue Sky had sent men around the canyon, but the men had returned, telling him it was impossible to launch any form of attack from above the people in the canyon. The sides were too steep and the rim straight vertical. With this information, Blue Sky decided to wait. Time was the weapon now. Time for the people inside to run out of food. Time for their bellies to swell and their strength to ebb, and then he would attack with all his men.

Blue Sky ordered more permanent shelters to be made, and the men to rest and prepare new arrows. Others he sent out to hunt and bring back game. But he also ordered guards to be posted at all times. There had been several strange happenings. Two braves had been found dead over the past several days. Their throats had been cut with one clean swift blow, and their knives and bows taken. From the canyon the people must have a very good brave, able to sneak out and kill his men in their sleep.

From a small vantage point, Shining Moon sat and watched the invaders. This, his third day, he knew now the sight of the chief. If only he could kill the chief. It would break the will of the invaders, and they would go from the land and his people would be safe. Over the past days he did not think much about Flying Bird. There was no room in his life for love or soft things. He only thought of killing and revenge for the crimes against his people. Already two fresh scalps hung from the braid of his pony. But he was also wary. He knew at any minute he could be discovered and killed. But now he would not kill the braves but would wait and watch and in time he would kill the chief. It would be strong medicine to have the spirit of the chief. But it was not medicine Shining Moon was after. He wished to quell the hate that filled his heart. To kill the man responsible for separating him from his love.

CHAPTER 8
INSIDE THE CANYON

Inside the canyon all was not well. After ten suns, the food was growing short and several attempts by braves to sneak out of the canyon and through the enemy in search of food had met with the death of the braves. There were only ten horses left, all the others had been eaten. And now there were only several suns left of corn. Black Bison could see the look of hunger and despair on his people, but still there was no vision to Man of Darkness. At night, sitting alone, Black Bison would sit and try to come up with some idea. There had to be a way. He could not let his people starve. But he could also not let his people become slaves. Of his 100 warriors he now had sixty left, but they were in short supply of arrows. He knew the enemy had suffered far more deaths, but they were outside with the food and wood. The people could not hold out much longer. Black Bison was alone in his despair and the cries of his people.

Flying Bird in her hunger with each passing day became delirious. Now she could see nothing but Shining Moon's face around her. She would sit and talk to the image. Telling him of her love. She could feel his touch, and at times could feel the life of a child inside her womb. Sleeping Bear and Mother and Grandmother could do nothing for the girl. It was as though her life had lost its spirit and the gods were slowly taking her away.

This night Man of Darkness still did not have a vision. There was nothing but the darkening and ever-increasing sense of cold and desolation that blanketed him. Even the touch of his wife did not bring him joy.

Black Bison sat with the night and prayed, but even his prayers gave him no peace. He could see the end, and in a strange manner, he began to welcome the feeling.

CHAPTER 9
THE SACRIFICE

Shining Moon over the past nights had not gone in to kill the enemy but stayed far away, waiting for his opportunity. Deep inside himself he knew he would die, and with this thought he slowly went over his life. The deep love he felt for Flying Bird took over all his power. It was as though he was no longer himself, but was his woman. His mind, his body, his soul were hers. In his chest her heart throbbed. In his veins her blood flowed. He would sit at night holding the spear point in his hands and he could feel the caress of Flying Bird. He could hear her sing with the stars and feel her breath upon his lips. The feelings were so strong he was not sad but completely engulfed by her love. And in his feeling he knew the gods would take him, and he knew the gods would forever watch over Flying Bird. He also knew that in the life after they would be together. They would be the song of the river, the flutter of fall leaves, the first snow of winter. They would be in all things. A testimony to the good of life, a beginning for each day and a hope for all tomorrows. For two more days Shining Moon sat and meditated. He gathered his strength and waited.

Inside the canyon Black Bison knew the end was near, and calling his warriors together it was decided that soon, instead of surrendering, they would kill their own people and then kill themselves. It was better to die as a people than be one with the enemy. The warriors were silent, thinking of the day to come and all in their heart sang their death song.

The next day Black Bison walked amongst his people and his heart was like stone. There was no earth, no sky, only sadness and deep grief around him.

Shining Moon with the dark crept towards the enemy camp. He had taken the earth and rubbed it over his body. He wore nothing but a loin cloth and carried nothing but a knife and the spear point tied to his side. With each passing moment he crept closer. Soon he was inside the perimeter of the guards. And within 100 paces of the chief. Creeping closer and closer he could hear his heart pound in his chest and when he was within ten paces of the chief, sitting by his fire, Shining Moon sprang from the ground, and yelling he ran and plunged his knife deep into the heart of the chief. Blue Sky would not have a last thought. Would not be able to sing his death song. He would only feel the first initial pain of the wound until he fell face forward to the earth and death.

Immediately braves jumped on Shining Moon and tore into his body with knives and lances. One lance severed the cord that held the pouch with the spear point and it fell to the earth. More braves appeared and seeing their dead leader continued to stab and mutilate the body of Shining Moon. In their anger their feet stomped the ground around Shining Moon, burying into the earth the beautiful spear point that spoke of love and hope. When the braves' frenzy was over, no man could tell who Shining Moon was or ever had been. With this, the braves looked at their leader. Inside of them the magic was gone. The gods had deserted them. And before the sun rose they mounted their ponies and departed the canyon to head south once again, taking their chief with them.

When the sun rose, braves at the mouth of the canyon noticed there was no smoke from the enemy's camp, and one, acting on his own, ran towards the enemy. Standing in their camp he saw only the mutilated cut up body of an Indian, but he did not know who it was or why it was there. But the invaders were gone, and he let out a deep cry of joy that brought the other braves running from the canyon. Soon the entire tribe was awake and staggering out into the world.

Ten moons later, the people had returned to the pueblo. They left the canyon, burying all the dead from both sides. No one had ever discovered why the invaders had suddenly left but it was known that Shining Moon had never returned to the people. Many believed he had been captured and killed trying to break through the invaders to reach the people. Flying Bird would not speak for several months. Her life, a dark world with no sunshine or bird song.

But late one evening she would have a vision that Shining Moon was riding a pony across a vast green field and he was singing her name. "My love, my love," he spoke, "we will have our time."

The following year she would marry a fine young man, a man who made bows but was not a warrior, and they would have three children. But Flying Bird would never forget Shining Moon, and would dream forever of her death and the afterworld when she would be with him. And in times of sadness she would take from a small wooden box lined in rabbit fur two small turquoise earrings, and remember his touch upon her trembling skin.

In front of the box canyon the rain would come and the wind would blow and the seasons would pass, and the obsidian spear point filled with love and life, still razor sharp, would wait. Wait for another hand and another time.

And the land would be as it had been for as long as the Indian could remember.

BOOK TWO
THE SPANIARDS

After their inital impact into the Southwest, the Spanish would be repulsed by the Indians and sent running back to Mexico — but they would stubbornly return in their greed for gold and silver. Besides gold and silver, they also came into the land with priests to bring the true God to the heathens. The gold and silver they would never find in the the quantities they sought, but the impact of the priests would remain to this day.

CHAPTER 1
THE FRANCISCAN - 1740 A.D.

Father Perez del Nuevo Majico slid wearily from his horse and tied the rope from his burro to the saddle. It had been a hard long ride this day. He stretched his short weary body and plopped down on the ground and began to rub his tired legs. Making the sign of the cross, he looked up at the clear blue sky and made a slightly embarrassed face. "Dear God," he spoke, "I know I have vowed poverty but now I would love to be sitting in a cool place with a bottle of burgundy." The priest stood and looked out across the desolate land before him. There were no tall stately trees, no shade for miles. On the horizon shimmering in the summer heat sat the mountains and just before that, the Spanish garrison and pueblo. In the mountains Majico knew grew tall trees and between the trees mountain springs ran with cool clear water.

Majico stood on the edge of a slowly sloping mesa. Below him he could see the tumbling mud walls of an old Indian pueblo, and for several moments he stood and contemplated the swiftness of time. For the individual to feel so important had always mystified Majico. It was very hard to feel secure in life, and Majico pictured how man could go through his days without knowing there was a God. Looking down upon the ruined village, Majico wondered what life had gone on there. He could see small Indian children playing in the ruined courtyards and men and women walking about discussing the weather and crops. Out beyond the ruin men would have been training horses and playing games. And somewhere years earlier there had been lovers. Men and women who looked into each other's eyes and thought of children and hope — so in love they did not see time in front of them, only today. And for a moment Majico's heart swelled in his chest and a small tear formed in his eye. He caught the feeling and rubbed his eye and took a deep breath. But getting back on his horse and forcing the burro to follow with stiff tugs on the rope, he could not help but see her face and feel saddened once again.

Majico did not know that the ghosts of Sleeping Bear and Flying Bird, Black Bison and Shining Moon were in the ruins he rode towards. He did not know that after the battle, Man of Darkness's dream would come true. That within sixty years the people would be driven out of their home by the returning Spanish. Unable to stay hidden, unable to stop progress. They had melted into other Indian tribes of the area. Some going south, others north, and still others to live alone. Black Bison's people were no more. They were but lost memories with no written history to tell of their deeds or lives. Majico rode and the fine brown dust of the earth made tiny puffs from the horse's feet. He was very weary. It had been a long hard ride from Chihuahua, Mexico, to this place.

At first there had been four of them. Four young brave priests with God in their hearts ready to go forth and bring to the heathens the true word. Bring Salvation to the wilderness. It was a grand quest. One Majico had given all of his life for. One that was not a mere compulsion but a drive far more powerful than life or love that swept through his body. They had been blessed by the bishop and sent out into the wilderness. The first days, nothing dampened their spirits. At night they would camp and eat and then pray and talk of the deeds they would do. The souls they would save. And they would dream about the Indians and the strange tales they had heard. They were not afraid but blessed by their God. Many priests had gone before them and many had died in their seeking. Thrown from cliffs by unthankful savages, martyred for their God. Each man knew this, but each also knew if he died he would be close to his God. Their sacrifice would not be in vain.

Each day of their travel brought them new sights, new sounds, new hopes, but in the third week, rising with the dawn, they had been surrounded by savage Indians. Majico had hidden in the rocks as his three friends were killed. Their screams of agony would forever fill his heart.

And he would know why he was not found and also killed. God must surely have blessed him. There was a destiny he must follow. After the Indians had gone. Majico had buried his brothers and left the spot on one lone horse that also had escaped, and a small skinny burro. With him he had only a few pots and pans, his rosary and silver chalice, and several small loaves of bread. From that day forth in his travels he looked for a sign. God must surely guide him and give him a sign. And in his grief, Majico began to draw pictures in his mind of the church he would build. A church in the wilderness that in time would overflow with the souls of the heathen.

But each continuing day became harder and harder. And soon Majico was eating anything he could find. He sucked the moisture from the tall yucca plant, he ate grasshoppers and black bugs that crawled along the desert floor. He captured lizards and roasted them over a tiny fire. But he never lost his faith or his love for his God. There was no sacrifice too large to deviate him from his calling in life. No hardship he could not withstand.

Majico stopped his horse in the middle of the Indian ruin. It was a strange place, the ruin. For a moment he did not dismount but sat and a warm deep feeling came over him. A feeling as deep as her touch had been. A feeling as deep as any God could place upon a man, and Majico closed his eyes and felt the desert wind move lightly over his face and his mind and heart went back to his beloved Spain and the tiny village he had been born in. And as if by magic, he could see her in her house busy making dinner. Two children ran around her legs and she was smiling.

Majico opened his eyes and smiled and slid from the horse. Looking around him he saw in the distance a strange peak that rose out of the rolling dry land. And he thought God's hands surely made that peak. And he knew after all the weeks, after all the hardship, he had found the place for his church. Not far away was the Indian pueblo and Spanish garrison. But here, beside this ruin, he would build his church. Here, next to man's mortality. Here the savages would come to him. And Majico knelt down upon the earth and prayed. "Father in heaven, He who has taken me through the wilderness, He who has brought me to this spot, guide and protect me in all things," and with a pause he spoke, "And watch over her, my God — she is true and good of heart."

Majico stood and looked at his new home. Not far away on the horizon he could see the tall green cottonwoods of the settlement. Not more than a half hour's ride away. Majico was overjoyed when he found the small stream surrounded by overgrown salt cedars behind the ruin, and he could picture in time tall cottonwoods here and a pond for his sheep and goats. And with excitement he began to move rapidly around the ruin. Scattered everywhere were pieces of broken pottery, red and black, off greens and purples, and he marveled at the work, picking up the broken pieces and holding them in his hand. Once a woman had modeled these into large pots and containers. And he could feel the heart of man in the broken sherds. Here was life and time and love. Here in the tiny pieces of broken clay was the true essence of man. All man, savage and God-fearing. To Majico, man was good of nature. He did not tell this to many people in fear of rebuttal. To the church, man was born of sin, but Majico had never believed this. Man was born pure and clean; it was life and time that brought him to sin. God would never allow his people to be born with a mark against them because of the actions of another man. Majico picked up a stick and, going by the river, he drew in the soft dirt a large square. This would be his church, this would be his life's work. Sitting down in the middle of his square, Majico was so overcome with joy, tears began to run down his face and he did not try to stop the torrent. His tears would be the foundation of his church.

That evening Majico made a crude shelter inside one of the ruins that had not completely fallen down, and slept soundly, refreshed by the cool water and the peace in his heart. In the morning he rose early and taking his horse and burro, he slowly walked towards the tall cottonwood trees and his first sight of a man in weeks.

Surrounded by the cottonwoods was a small Spanish garrison of twenty-six men. Behind the garrison was a medium-sized pueblo with more than 300 hundred Indians. In this pueblo were descendants of Flying Bird, but they did not know this. From the garrison, the twenty-six men were supposed to keep the peace of the area and stay in contact with the settlement of Santa Fe 26 miles away. This task impossible, they mostly played cards, drank their homemade liquor, and did nothing.

The man in charge, Hernan Aguirre, was not a bad man, but he also was not a good man. He was a military man with orders from the king of Spain to keep the peace, and this he did with harsh judgments at any transgression. It was not uncommon to beat the Indians or hang them for minor offenses. Only through strength was man taught, he believed and lived by. From the Indians, the Spaniards received all things — corn, maize, meat, blankets and women. Already over the past years there were many children running around with the blue eyes of the Spaniards. But the Spaniards did not marry the Indian women. They had wives back in Spain and children, true women of the word, not heathens or savages. At all times the Spaniards felt superior to the Indian. Not knowing that the Indian had established a culture long before there was culture in Spain. Not knowing the Indian had learned to live with his land and earth. The Indians of the pueblo on the whole were a peaceful, placid lot, growing crops and raising goats and sheep and turkeys. As long as the chief held his control there was no problem.

Hernan Aguirre sat in a rough one-room adobe and sipped from a bottle of wine. Scattered across his desk were many papers, none in order. The latest paper he had received from the chancellor in Mexico told him of four priests who would arrive to build a church and that the soldiers would help them build it. Aguirre screwed his face up in a grimace when he received the letter. God, he thought, all I need is a bunch of God's men in my way. To Aguirre there might have been a God, but He was nothing he could touch or see or feel. So God was not important. Over the weeks no priests had arrived and he had forgotten the letter. Now he was mostly concerned about several young bucks in the pueblo who had been causing trouble, trying to talk the pueblo into revolt against the Spaniards. He had several good spies in the pueblo, men won over by liquor who told him many things. But Aguirre knew if there was an uprising, he must be prepared or they could not withstand the rush of people. He kept his three cannons aimed directly at the chief's home at all times and at the slightest indication of trouble, the people and the chief knew, he would light the fuses with no qualms. Mostly Hernan Aguirre was bitter and disgusted. He was far too great a man to be placed in the wilderness with a bunch of brown heathens. By now the king should know all the stories of gold cities were but fables and send him back to Spain and give him an important position. His men were a sorry, lazy lot, content in cheating the Indians and playing cards.

Hernan Aguirre rose from his desk and went out into the warm day, and this was the first time he saw Father Majico as he rode into the garrison. He looked at the short, fat little man with the round perspiring face and deep-set eyes filled with God and conviction, and his stomach turned. Lord, he thought, walking to the dismounting priest, he made it.

Father Majico smiled broadly seeing the Spanish captain. The captain smiled back and held out his hand. "I am glad you arrived safely," he lied. "Messages of your coming arrived weeks ago." Remembering his comrades, the priest almost let a tear fall from his eye, but he said nothing except, "I was chosen while others were not."

Sitting in the captain's office drinking a glass of wine, the little priest smiled. "It is indeed a glorious day, my friend," he spoke, " a very glorious day." The captain looked at the little man and deep within himself he knew that hidden behind the plump round face was a very brave and strong man.

CHAPTER 2
THE CHURCH

After spending a comfortable night with the captain, Majico left in the morning with fifteen Indians and six soldiers. On his burro was food and wine for himself. It was a glorious day to Majico, leading the small procession of men towards his new church. The Indians and the men were going to build the church, forming out of the earth the adobe blocks that would go one on top of the other until the structure was completed. How fitting, Majico thought, to build from the earth a temple for the heavens. Majico had always felt close to the earth. Seeing in all living things the true heart of God, seeing a spirit that filled life with hope. To him all things could be rationalized in God's love. There was nothing God did not know or see or make happen. It was not always good for man, but man did not know what God had in store for him. This Majico believed with all his heart and soul. In this he had to believe or forever lose his faith.

Even as a child, Majico knew he would be a man of the cloth. From the time he was six he had read and studied the Bible. There was nothing God was not responsible for. When he was fourteen he had gone to the abbey and started his formal training, choosing to become a priest and go out into the world. It had all been easy for him.

But when he was twenty-two he had been sent from the abbey to go into town and buy bread for dinner. Walking down the street in his brown robe, he had felt proud and alive. It was a warm summer day. There was not a care in the world in Majico's heart. But it was then that he saw her, and it was as though all life had been taken from his body. There was not a living creature in the world as beautiful as she. Majico had stopped and his eyes had swept frantically over the girl. She was not tall, five feet one-inch or two, but her face was as the Madonna. Her eyes shone with purity and grace, and her lips were like small delicate red roses. Her hair flowed down upon her shoulders in dark rivulets. She wore a white cotton blouse, loose-fitting but not loose enough so that Majico could not see the tiny points of her breasts gently touching the fabric and a dark skirt that molded around her delicate rounded hips. Majico watched as she entered the baker's shop and, in a trance, he followed her inside.

Standing in line with others for bread, he was directly behind her. He could smell the fragrance of her skin and the odor her hair gave off. Surely she is a nobleman's daughter, he thought. But then he knew she must be a maid, or she would not be there to buy bread.

It was then a man in back of him bumped into him, and Majico was pushed into the back of the girl. Clumsily he grabbed her arms and held her from falling. The girl, startled, turned abruptly upon regaining her balance, and as she did, her hair spun with her and swept across Majico's face. The look of anger that had been on her face vanished immediately when she saw the young priest, and a large, delicate smile spread across her lips, exposing the tiny tip of her pink tongue.

Majico gazed deeply into her eyes, and here he knew was God, the true God, resting in the soul of this girl. Majico tried to speak, but there were no words and the girl smiled and turned once more, facing the man in front of her. After the girl bought her bread, she turned, and passing Majico she smiled once again and was gone.

Majico stood looking at the baker, and he did not know where he was. No sound came into his voice. There was only a ringing in his ears and the roar of his heart that he knew for sure could be heard around the store. The baker looking at the young priest grew impatient. "What is it young priest?" he spoke harshly. Majico shook his head and in a stammering voice gave his order.

That night, lying on his cot after benediction, Majico could not sleep. The vision of the girl swam in front of his face like the stars. He would shut his eyes and try to chase her sight away, but there was only the touch of her hair and the outline of her small delicate breasts before him. And for the first time in his life, Majico felt passion grow up inside himself and he was uncomfortable.

As the days passed, Majico could not chase the memory from his mind, and his days were long and tiresome in his tumult. The next Sunday as the priests filed into the church and their normal pews, Majico saw the girl standing in the aisle, helping an old woman to sit down. And once again his heart was alive, and he wanted to bolt from the line of priest and run to her side and bend down on his knees before her. There was nothing in the world as she, nothing in life, and sitting through the mass Majico was lost and a cold numbing feeling crept over his heart. That night in bed he prayed: Dear God, why? Take from me these feelings, remove from my sight the vision of the girl. I who have followed you truthfully do not wish this test. But the prayer did not work, and the look of the girl swam in front of him still.

The Indian men and soldiers watched the priest as he rode. To the Indians he did not seem like much of a man. But as of yet, they had not been cornered by the zeal and strength of the priest. In their hearts there was a religion, a religion of the earth and the spirits. Many gods, many truths. Their simple aspect of life was yet to be troubled by new gods, heavens and hells.

To the soldiers he was a man of God, and now they must do their whoring with the Indian women discreetly. And all men knew they must come to the church on Sunday. Having a priest around was like having a nagging wife.

Majico stopped the horse by the ruins and tiny stream and pointed with his finger. "Here, my friends," he spoke, "here is where my church will be." The soldiers spoke nothing, but thought of the work hauling the water and stacking the adobe bricks high into the sky.

That night after working all afternoon digging footings for the church, Majico lay in his crude shelter and he could hear the sounds of the soldiers and the few unintelligble words of the Indians. Lying there he could not sleep, and he rose and went outside into the dark. Overhead were millions and millions of stars and basking in the glow of the moon, Devil's peak loomed on the horizon. Majico was drawn to the peak by some unseen force, and as he stood gazing onto its form once again, a sharp pang of pain entered his heart. He could feel her breasts as they molded into his side, and taste the salt-sea taste of her lips as they kissed between their tears. He could hear her soft sighs as they lay together and feel the warmth of her nakedness against his skin. Majico slowly closed his eyes and placed his hands together. The memories — the warm memories.

In the morning work resumed at dawn after a breakfast of corn tortillas and goat. The little priest worked as hard as any man, talking and laughing, lifting the water and the mud. By noon countless adobe bricks lay out in the sun, growing hard as they dried. The soldiers began to like the little man. Most men of cloth would not work. Work was only preaching of God and giving communion. They all looked into his face and prayed that he would not remember their voices when it came time for confession. The Indians did not think about the strange man in brown robes. Only thinking he was foolish to wear such strange garb. But they also did not dislike him. By sundown the number of bricks had doubled and Majico stood and looked at the lines of bricks lying in neat rows along the ground, and in his mind's eye he could see the church rising out of the floor of the wilderness.

That evening as the sun set, Majico walked out away from the talking soldiers and stood by a twisted and gnarled cedar tree. The land was silent. Not a breeze moved, nor a creature scurried. Here alone Majico felt surrounded by his God. And he stood for several hours unmoving, listening, and feeling the glow of life around him.

After a week the adobes were done and within another two weeks the small adobe church stood. With this Majico made the Indians and the soldiers kneel down. The Indians did it for no reason; the Spaniards for their souls.

"Dear God," Majico's voice spoke to the sky, "here is our testimony to our love and hope, here is proof of our faith in your divine sight and judgment. Bless us all this day and let us in your wisdom guide the unknowing in the path of truth." With this the Indians filed back to the pueblo and the soldiers rode back with instructions that church would be on Sunday and all men would be seen there.

After the men had gone, Majico looked at his church and ran his hands over the worked earth. It was a beautiful structure. A place fresh and clean. Inside he himself would make the altar from split cedar. Majico walked to his shelter and taking his pack with trembling hands pulled out the silver chalice. "Life of God," he spoke looking into the silver, "your blood runs through my veins."

The chalice placed on a log in front of the church, Majico went outside and, kneeling, faced the west. "Carmeleta, my love," he spoke, "I have built my church." And far away across the ocean, a lady smiled and made the sign of the cross as she did each day as the sun set, and prayed for a little round plump priest.

CHAPTER 3
THE PEAK

For the remainder of the week Majico cut and trimmed cedar trees. Cutting the hard cedar wood planks within a few days he had a beautiful cedar altar. Next he worked on a box for the chalice, and then he made a crude crucifix of cedar branches. Standing in his church with no windows but light from the roughed out cedar door, he was filled with love for all mankind. His church was indeed a true church. Not a church of Spain or Mexico filled with gold and silver and stained glass windows made by well-paid artists. His was a true church, the true home of God. His church was made from the earth. It was not made by artists but by man, normal, hard-working man. And to Majico this small brown adobe church was the finest church in the world. A true image of God the Father.

As Majico worked he was carried away with his passion. He would breathe and the dirt smell of the church would fill his nostrils, and he could not help but be filled with his belief. With the church complete, Majico could concentrate on a house. He would build a small 15 foot by 15 foot adobe behind the church. He would not need anything else. He would make a bed and a praying stand and here he would be one with God. In time he would have the soldiers help him build pews for his church, but for now the people would stand. Standing and kneeling was not too much to ask in God's home.

Sunday morning Majico was excited. He stood outside his church and looked towards the garrison. By nine in the morning he saw the small dust cloud that followed the mounted Spanish towards the church. At ten when church started, there were nineteen men from the garrison, from which he had heard eight quick confessions, and there were also twenty-one Indians, two of whom were drunk. But the condition of his worshippers in no way dented Majico's enthusiasm.

The mass over, he looked at the people filing out of the church and he was amazed for the first time at the lack of women. He had never thought about that before. But in the corners of the world there were very few women. And for a moment he felt sorry for the men. Living without love was a great sacrifice.

Standing outside as the column of men grew smaller and

smaller on the horizon, Majico felt a great sadness come over him. But instead of fighting the feeling, he let it sweep over his body and mind like a gentle breeze, and closing his eyes he could see Carmeleta holding her two small children by their hands and leading them up the marble steps of the church back home. Behind them was her husband. A fine strong bricklayer. "My love, my love," he murmured to the bright day. "Would that I could see you again." And for a brief moment his soul seemed to lift from his body, and he was high in the rafters of the church, back in Spain, and he could look down and see the black lace kerchief Carmeleta wore, and he could smell her jasmine perfume from behind her ear. In her delicate hands she held her prayer book and he knew, as with each sundown and every Sunday, she would say a prayer to St. Christopher to protect Majico. Majico gathered his thoughts and walked around to the corral he had built. He saddled his horse slowly. It was a good day for a ride.

Majico rode towards the tall table-topped peak not too far away. Through conversations with the men from the garrison, he had learned that to the Indians the rock was evil. But Majico knew an object could not be evil. Man was the only creature that could be evil. Riding, Majico was overwhelmed by the distance around him. Here one could sit and look out over the land and see three shimmering mountain ranges in the distance. One to the west, one to the east and one to the north. Only south did the land lie without an image in the distance. It seemed like a time-immortal place. Unchanged for eons and eons, a resting place for the earth, unmovable. But Majico knew like all things even the land changed. Maybe at a different time level, but all things changed. Majico rode and he thought about his trip through the wilderness and his little church by the ruin, and once again his mind returned to his home far across the ocean and Carmeleta.

It was a Friday morning in the middle of summer and Majico was once again in town. The priests were trying to raise money for a family in need and Majico was sent door to door to ask for any donations. After many houses he was quite discouraged over the meager amount of money he had been given. Did not people know they were their brother's keeper? Did they not know God would surely punish their miserliness? He was on a small back street of the town. A clean street with fine and well-kept houses. Knocking on the next door, a tall well-dressed man answered and looked at him gruffly. "Priests," he snorted, "asking for more money, I suppose."

suppose."

Majico did not speak but started to walk away. Some souls were not worth redeeming. As he turned, the man touched his shoulder. "Go to the side door, Father, I know my religious helpers would be more than happy to assist you."

Majico walked around the side of the house and knocked on the door. He had never understood servants or a man's wish for servants. Every man should do his own work. Work was the gift of God, the redemption of the soul, the cleanser of the body. Knocking on the door Majico was looking at a beautiful geranium that bloomed deep crimson red in the window beside the door. He was not looking when she opened the door, but when the door creaked he turned and she was there. He felt his heart turn and his legs grow weak, and standing with the soft glow of the sun he saw the girl's cheek turn pink.

Majico stammered trying for words, but he could only stand and look upon the girl. Once again his gaze was pulled into her eyes, and once again he could smell the fresh spring scent of her hair. The girl looked at the little short pudgy priest and smiled. "Father," she spoke with the voice of a songbird, "we meet once again."

Majico smiled deeply and without thought spoke, "You are as lovely as the summer."

The girl felt a deep warm glow spread across her bosom and a slight tingling come to her toes. With a pause that seemed like eternity, she stood silent and then spoke, "Come in, good priest, come in. What brings you to this home?"

Majico entered the large kitchen. There were several women peeling potatoes and others running around shouting and giving orders. "Hurry, hurry, the people will be here and we will not be done." Before he knew it, the girl had taken his hand and led him to a corner of the kitchen and sat him down in a large wooden chair. "Sit here. I will bring you something to drink."

Sitting, Majico watched the girl walk away, and his heart sank, she was so lovely, so very very lovely. Returning, the girl set before him a cup of tea and a sweet pastry. "Here," she spoke, and sat down beside him in another chair. Majico sipped the tea, groping for words. He wanted to reach out and touch the girl. Feel the touch of her fingers on his brow. But gathering his thoughts, he spoke, not looking at the girl.

"I am seeking donations for a family in need outside of town.

The husband was killed and the wife and five children are starving."

A sadness seemed to sweep across the girl's face and she stood and spoke loudly above the noise of the kitchen. "Listen, the priest needs money for a family in need." With a hush, all the people came over to the priest and each in turn gave him money from their pockets and folds of their dresses.

The girl left for a moment and returned, giving Majico many coins. "I am sorry," she spoke, but this is all I have. Majico was touched by the people's generosity and he knew none of them could afford to give away as much as they did. He put the money in his leather money pouch and hid it in the folds of his brown frock. Standing, the girl rose with him and walked him to the door. By the door he turned and looked at the girl. "What is your name?" he asked tentatively. The girl looked deep into his eyes and spoke, "Carmeleta, my priest." Majico turned and walking away murmured, "I will pray for you, little one."

For the rest of the day Majico was not conscious of the doors he knocked on or the money he gathered. There was only the name Carmeleta that rested in his mind and sent his body reeling in emotions and dreams.

Majico lost his thoughts when the horse stumbled slightly on a rock. Shaking his head, he made the sign of the cross and blinked his eyes several times. He was amazed, but he was within a hundred yards of the table-top peak, and for no reason a rush of excitement swept through his body. Dismounting he led the horse the remainder of the way to the peak, and tying the horse to a gnarled pinon tree, he stepped up to the peak. A great wave of feelings poured through his body at the first sighting of the many faces that were etched into the ageless rock. Here were faces smiling, some frowning, here were little men playing a flute-like instrument with hunched backs. And here also were deer and bison, rabbits and lizards. Wrapped around one edifice of the rock was a serpent over eight feet long. Majico stood and it was as though time reached out and grasped his heart. Here was man, man as he — ancient man, seeking, pulling out from within themselves the search for immortality. This was not an evil place. This was a place of good and beauty, a place where man could stand and see the immensity of life around him. Here was a place man was belittled by all of God's creation. Here was the truth of the Lord.

Majico slowly walked around the base of the peak which was

no more than 30 yards in circumference. Coming around a large outcropping he came to the most beautiful pictograph of all. Here was a horse. A large horse galloping. His mane swept back as though the living wind was upon the rock. His hooves flew through the air. And Majico stood and he could see a man standing in deep thought, slowly scraping away the rock, putting his life and his blood into his drawing. He could see a man speaking through his art, telling the future, I am, I was, I will be. And he could picture the man working and stepping back from his work, inspecting, making if all possible the lines just as he wished. And when he was finished he could see the man smile, knowing throughout time he would live on this rock. Come whatever there would be a testimony to his being. And Majico knew that surely God, too, had been with the ancient man. The older Majico grew, the more he knew God was in many forms. He could not believe God was only a Catholic. There had always been God. God speaking to his most beautiful creation in a way they would understand. Surely this man had known God. God had sat and watched him work. A work as beautiful as this horse had to be inspired by a deep love and God. With this Majico bent down and picked up a rock and he scratched into the rock above the horse a simple cross.

After this Majico stood for many hours looking at the etchings. Rivers of thought swept over him, feelings that at times made him cold and other times made him sweat. From the peak Majico could turn and see his tiny church in the distance and could make out the falling mud walls of the Indian ruins. And he knew that one day a man would stand here, and he would see Majico's church crumbled in ruin. And the man would wonder what life went on here, what dreams were carried out and what dreams were shattered within the tumbling walls. With this, Majico fell to his knees and picking up a handful of earth, bowed his head and prayed. "Dear Lord Jesus, I am but a man created from the earth I hold in my hand. Make of me as this rock and give me the strength to continue in my task."

CHAPTER 4
TROUBLE

Hernan Aguirre scowled deeply and looked at the small shrunken Indian before him. The man disgusted him. His brown skin fell in folds over his face and his clothes were dirty and grimy. It was strange what alcohol did to these people. It was worse than opium or hash. And although deep inside himself the captain hated traitors, he needed spies like this to maintain his control over the people. Although he and his men were far superior in mind, he also knew they were greatly outnumbered, and without prior notification they could be wiped out in an instant. The captain was not a priest and martyrdom to him was not salvation.

Rain Tree sat, his red glazed eyes trying to focus on the captain. In his mind there was no world now. Just the need of his pain-wracked body for alcohol. He did not feel grief or sadness over coming to the captain. He felt only need and compulsion for the oblivion alcohol brought to his mind. There was nothing else in life. He was no longer an Indian, he was no longer a man, he just was, a thing lost to the world and to his spirit.

"How many of these young men are there?" the captain spoke sitting down at his desk.

Rain Tree rolled his head and stammered over thirty that he knew of. The captain strummed the top of his desk with his fingers. "Thirty," he mused, that was bad. "And tell me what they say, Rain Tree."

Rain Tree ran his filthy hands through his long snarled hair. Rain Tree looked longingly at the whiskey bottle on the captain's desk, and the captain poured a small shot and handed it to him. Smacking his lips his eyes seemed to focus for a moment before returning to a glazed stupored look. And he began to speak. "They meet secretly away from the eyes of the chief and elders. They are all young men, brave men, and hate you. They talk of stealing in with the night and cutting your throats, taking your horses and your cannons. They say you are bad men and only have evil in your heart. They speak of your search for the yellow rock. Their leader is Jagged Knife. You will know him as he has a large scar across his face from a battle with your people several years ago. He, of all men, hates your people the most. He has dreams and tells the people of his dreams. In his dreams you have trampled the earth, our mother. And already he spreads stories about the little man who lives by the old ruin. Your man of your God. He tells the people this man will come to them and tell them of different gods and that surely as he speaks of his God, our gods will turn from us and we will be wiped out like so many of the other tribes." The captain stood and taking the bottle of whiskey handed it to the Indian. Rain Tree rose and grasped the bottle with trembling hands and left the office clutching the bottle like it was his redemption.

The captain paced around his tiny office. This was such a desolate place, dry and windblown, filled with cactus and snakes. The Indians were scum, believing in many gods, believing in dreams and strange ceremonies. And he was here trying to survive. If nothing else he must survive. If it meant he had to wipe out the complete Indian pueblo, he would survive. Hernan Aguirre turned and walked briskly towards the billets of the men. He would put them on alert, at all times there would be men with their guns ready for any happening. He had already been here for four years. It could not be that long before they would call him back to Mexico and then back to Spain. Living with these heathens was driving him insane.

Jagged Knife walked quickly down the street of the pueblo. Around him the multi-storied adobe buildings teamed with life. Dogs ran and barked amongst half-naked playing children. Women haggled and bartered over blankets and corn, chickens and turkeys. Old men sat in circles throwing gaming pieces. Jagged Knife loved this place. There was no other world to him. But deep inside himself he seethed with hatred. He hated the chief and the elders and the medicine men who told the people to ignore the Spaniards, and at times he even hated the people for listening to their leaders. But most of all he hated the Spaniards. The strange men who had come into the land before his birth. Killing and torturing people. Did not the people understand? This was their land, their home. This was where the gods had chosen for them to live. Live alone with the sky and the birds, the wind. The distant mountains. Here the people took only what they needed. Jagged Knife turned a corner and ducked into a small narrow doorway. Inside the room it was dark and cool. His eyes adjusting to the dark, he saw the faces of all his friends. His followers. He knew he was the catalyst that held the group together. Without him they would be only a mob with no direction. He gave them a force. His words molded them into action. Jagged Knife smiled deeply at his followers. They were all the young men. In their late teens and early twenties. Brave men who believed in freedom and themselves. Not old men like the elders and medicine men. Old men who sat complacently while the people slowly degenerated. Speaking of time and wisdom. Telling the people it must be the gods' will that the brown people had come and that the gods would surely drive the people from their land. Jagged Knife believed in the gods there was no doubt, but he also believed man was the true God. Man's actions alone made man what he was. God was a part of the man, not the whole. If not, why else did man love and need, desire and wish? Why must he grow corn and thirst and feel sorrow? Man was the creator of his destiny, not the product of it.

Jagged Knife stood in front of the group of men. One man stood outside the door looking for spies. Jagged Knife knew there were spies in the village. Old, weak people who had been seduced by the liquor of the Spaniards. People who, like women, ran to the Spaniards telling them of any happening that was not in accordance with the Spanish rules enforced upon the tribe. Revolt or thought of revolt was a serious crime and could lead to death or severe whipping. Jagged Knife looked out over the faces of his men and began to speak. "I have ridden to the pueblo to the north and found many men there who will join us. Already they prepare their ponies and weapons. Also to our west I have ridden and have recruited many men. With the passing days more and more of the people begin to hate the Spaniards. They see that all the Spaniards are evil. They have come and brought their diseases, killing our people like flies. They have brought their alcohol that sends our men into another world. They sleep with our women and bring children into the world that are neither themselves or us. The day draws near. We must prepare ourselves. But now is not the time. There are many spies and we must be wary of our words and meetings. The elders and the chiefs must not know about us. But when the day comes we will strike and all the brown men will be killed or driven away from our land and our people." The men sitting nodded and grunted in agreement. "But also we must not let the words of the priest from Mexico corrupt the minds of our people. I have seen men as he before. There have been many. They come telling of their strange god, a god who will send us to a burning place for all time if we do not accept him. These are strange men and in many ways are much stronger than the soldiers with their cannon and rifles. But we also cannot go out and kill the priest. If he died then surely the cannon will be fired into our village." Starting to walk away, Jagged Knife stopped by the door. "I will be back, I am going south to another pueblo, and once again we will meet."

Jagged Knife slipped through the doorway and walked briskly towards the south end of the pueblo. He did not see Rain Tree sitting in the darkened corner of another hut sipping the whiskey but Rain Tree saw him and the many faces that came from the door later. Rain Tree let his head fall to his chest and all around him was the darkness.

Jagged Knife trotted his horse for an hour and then slowed down to a walk. It would take him several days to reach the southern pueblo. Here also he knew he would find men for his cause. Right now the Spanish garrison was weak. They men complacent in their belief of strength. But he, Jagged Knife, would let them know his people were not weak. Jagged Knife could see himself killing the Spaniards. He could see their blood flowing onto the earth. Giving back to the mother that which they had taken. And during his ride and into the dark nights, the burning hatred fired in him like a smoldering ember.

Majico finished the last of the posts and stood back to look at his corral. He had built the corral so the tiny spring ran through the corner, forever stopping the chore of hauling water to the horse and burro. In one corner he had built a small coop for turkeys he would get from the Indians. Over the past weeks he had finished his house. And he felt very happy and carefree. Only recently had he begun to think about the souls of the Indians. Soon he must go to the pueblo and talk to the chief.

Walking out away from his church and corral and home, Majico turned and looked back at his tiny world. Seeing the work he smiled and looked towards the sky: Carmeleta, my love, my dream surrounds me.

CHAPTER 5
CARMELETA

Carmeleta rose early from bed. Her husband slept soundly, his snoring soft and muted by the pillow over his head. Putting on her robe she walked to the kitchen and started a small fire in the stove. She loved these times in the morning before her husband and children woke. She loved the way the fire started slowly and the creaks and groans of the stove. Always just before the sunrise there was a small brown sparrow that would chirp from the tree outside the kitchen window. It was such a small, lonely cry and touched Carmeleta deeply.

This morning Carmeleta went outside into the predawn. The eastern sky was a dull grey and as for now there was no definition of clouds. She rubbed her hands lightly through her hair and breathed deep the morning air. Today it had been ten years. It did not seem like ten years in her mind. She could still see Majico. He was such a funny looking little man. She would tell him he looked like a small brown ball in his frock. But although she would tell him he looked funny, inside she knew he was warm and good, as soft and gentle as the June rain.

She stood looking at the brightening horizon and wondered where he was this day. He had never written, telling her he would never do so. Telling her that his thoughts would forever be their book. Trying in a small way to ease both his pain and hers. But still she would look for a letter each day. But none ever came as she knew none ever would.

Carmeleta stood and remembered the first time she saw the funny priest. Standing in line to buy bread. She had seen him walking down the street and never in her young life had she felt such a feeling upon sight of a man. Being pretty there had never been a shortage of young men asking her out. Never a shortage of poems or pretty flowers placed by her window. But she had never felt a glow within her heart as when she saw Majico. Seeing him she had turned and stepped into line. With her back to the priest, she could hear his breathing as he stood, and smell the deep scent of incense on his robe. When he had fallen into her and his hands grabbed her arms, it was as though life itself was fully awakened in her body. Going from the bakery, he had not seen her turn and look at his back — had not known the burn that swept across her heart or felt the flutter of her fingers clutching the hard-crusted bread. He had not known how she lay in bed that night thinking about the priest or how her dreams came like demons to keep her tossing and turning through the night. But after several days she no longer had these feelings, and he no longer entered her mind.

It was not until mass and helping her grandmother into a pew that she saw him again. And even standing in the house of God, she could not control the wave of passion that swept through her body. Kneeling her head, bowed in prayer, she longed for the priest to be beside her. She wanted to feel the touch of his skin upon hers. And try as she may during mass she could not alter the thoughts that swept through her like fire.

The mass over, she sat and watched the priests file solemly out of the church, and for an instant Majico and her eyes locked across the expanse of the church, and it was as though they were one. One in the house of God. Walking slowly with her grandmother back to her grandmother's home, Carmeleta was silent. She had never seen the day as she saw this one. The people, colors and smells surrounded her. There was a clarity to the sky and everything in life seemed to be in rhythm. Leaving her grandmother she ran back to the house where she lived and worked and going into her room she lay down on the bed breathing deeply. "Dear God," she murmured through her small delicate lips, "why is it as such?"

Each day after that she could not lose the image of the priest. While she was cleaning, washing dishes or setting the master's table, he was there beside her. And her thoughts became very confused. He was not a handsome man. He was not a rich man. He was a man of God. A short little plump man with round arms and hands. Small beady eyes set deep within his pudgy face. But she did not see this. It was as though she saw Majico from the inside out. It was his heart that reached for her. His soul that came to her in the night as she lay in bed. And for the first time in her life, she wanted to be with a man. She wanted him inside her, safe and warm with her body. She wanted his hands to caress her skin and his lips to touch hers. But these thoughts only brought her agony. He was a man of God. A man pledged to a life of poverty and chastity. And she felt cheated in her feelings.

Once again Majico's thought left her mind, but then there came the day there was knock on the door, and even before Carmeleta opened the door, she knew the priest stood there. It was as though without sight she could see through the door. And when she opened the door and he stood there, she wanted to fly into his arms. Feel the coarseness of his gown against her. Tell him how deeply she longed for him. Tell him of her thoughts and desires. But she stood and smiled and watched as Majico stammered and tried to avoid her gaze. But she knew he felt for her as she felt for him, and she was warm and happy inside.

Sitting with the priest in the kitchen, it was as though she had known him forever. He was both a father and a brother to her. He was the blood of her body. There was nothing in her life he would not understand.

Carmeleta watched as the sun climbed above the horizon, spreading a golden glow upon the land. The lone sparrow's chirping was soon accompanied by many birds and down the street the roosters began to crow. Soon the peace would be gone and the town would be filled with the hustle and bustle of the day. Soon she would start breakfast and hug her children and kiss her husband as he went off to work. She had a good life and she loved her husband dearly. He was a strong hard-working good man. Not a true man of God, but a good man. He drank at times too much, but all men of toil needed drink. But he was good to the children and his complete life revolved around his family. Her children Carmeleta loved deeply. Both pretty little girls. They had eyes that sparkled and danced like their mother's, and small delicate lips that came easily into a smile.

Carmeleta stretched her arms above her head and her robe fell open and the morning breeze swept across the thin material of her night gown and it was as though Majico's hands had come with the day to caress her breasts. A light soft touch, a touch filled with joy and sadness. A caress she knew would never come again. Carmeleta pulled her robe around herself and sat down on a small bench that was in the front of the house.

How it had all come about she would never know. She did know that something as sweet and caring and beautiful as their love could not have come from the devil. She did know that in many ways God's will came into strange forms and shapes and surely Majico and she had been a part of God's plan for their lives.

After Majico had come for donations, it seemed that whenever she was in town she would see the little priest. They would meet and soon they would eat lunch, and then one afternoon they shared a glass of wine. From one happening to the next, it was as though they were pulled into each other. There was a loss of time and place. There was only the movement of the day, the passing of the hours, and then they would be back together once again. She would always remember what they talked about. He told her of his youth and she of hers. They talked about the sun and the stars. The trees and the birds, but they never talked of love. They never told each other of their feelings. They both knew their feelings. Their love for each other pulled them into each other's hearts. But despite their smiles and small talk, they both knew, but would not accept the fact, that they could never be. There would never be a home, or a garden. Never be children. There would never be a warm bed or many nights in each other's arms.

At times Majico would yearn so bad for her he would almost speak, "O, my love, my love. I will quit the church. We will be man and wife," but the words would never come and he could only look into her eyes and smile weakly. Too filled with emotion to speak. And there would be times Carmeleta would want to hear his voice say marry me, be mine, you are more important to me than life or God, but she knew that if she ever heard these words, she would tell him no. His life was God. There was nothing else. But in their feelings and longings, they did not run from each other. Neither was strong enough to wish to stop. Everything was too good, too warm, too peaceful to stop. But they knew there was a darkness to come in their lives.

After many weeks of seeing each other, they both chose a spot outside the town where they would meet. It was a soft quiet spot. A spot of trees and birds and a small pond covered with lilies. Here were frogs and dragon flies and bees. Here there was no world, just a time, a place to meet and talk and laugh and smile and feel sad.

It was late summer and the earth was in bloom when they met for the last time. Coming to the spot, Carmeleta saw Majico sitting, looking deep into the small pond. She sat down beside him, but he did not smile but reached out and for the first time he touched her face. Without speaking, he slowly traced the outline of her lips and the delicate roundness of her cheekbone. Then dropping his hand into his lap he told her. "I am going away, my love," and it was the first time he had ever called her in love's name. "Within a week I will sail for Mexico, and then from Mexico I will go into the wilderness to bring the heathens into the true word."

Carmeleta looked at the priest and great tears began to roll down her face. Tears that fell and stained the front of her blouse.

And Majico, with the touch of an angel, took the tears with his fingertips and touched them with the tears that creased his cheeks. Then with the summer breeze and the sound of the bees and the stillness of the pond, he stood and took off his frock and lay it down on the grass. Then slowly he took the clothes off Carmeleta and surrounded by heaven and earth, they became one.

They made love quietly and softly, bringing into their bodies all that each of them held within their hearts. Telling of the sadness and the love, telling of the fear of life and future. Telling that neither would ever forget, not with time, not with agony. And telling each other they would never be alone. No matter what life brought to them, they would always be one in spirit. When they lay spent and tired, eyes closed, they did not want to move from their embrace. They did not want to leave the confines of their arms. They lay kissing between the salt-sweet taste of their merging tears and tried to push away from their hearts the agony that would surely engulf them. In their embrace Carmeleta fell asleep. When she awoke, he was gone and she lay with the grass and the trees and the birds. Slowly dressing, it was as though her heart had been torn from her chest. Putting on her dress she felt the letter tucked into the small pocket, and taking it she could not open it but kissed the seal and held it close to her heart.

Majico had risen from the girl and stood. He had looked down and gazed at the curves of her body. Her breasts stood like small apples, red and full. Her thighs called to him. He looked at her neck and shoulders. He felt her knees and touched her toes. Forever he could see the girl and forever he would know she was God's creation. And never would he feel guilty about his love or his lying with Carmeleta. Through the girl he had touched the Lord. Nestled against her bosom, he had found true peace. She had been given as a gift by God to him. She had shown him the true path of man's love and forever in her absence he would love his Lord and keeper far deeper than he ever had.

And then, slipping away from his heart, he half-walked, half-ran back to the abbey. No priest would ever hear his confession. With her there had been no sin. With her there had only been happiness, and life, and the small place that was theirs alone with the trees and the pond and the bees. Forever it would be summertime when he recalled this day.

Falling to his knees by his bed, Majico crossed himself and buried his head on his coarse blanket. He could smell his love on his frock and he prayed: God in heaven, in my love there is no sin, in your gift of this feeling I love you deeper. And he stood and taking off his frock, he walked outside of the abbey and set it afire.

Carmeleta sat in her small room in the darkness holding the letter in her hands. With trembling fingers she lit the lamp on her table and opened the letter. Closing her eyes she took a deep breath before beginning to read.

My Dearest Lady: There is no time between you and I, we are and will always be one in our brief moments. Forever I walk in the beauty of your smile and in my thoughts and deeds you will rest. God has given us a great gift that will carry me through all the days of my life. I will never be able to write to you but each day I will pray for you. I wish for you the best in all you do and a love that keeps you warm during your life. You are a treasure in my life. The cornerstone of my soul. Without you there is no God. Majico.

And from the envelope fell a small gold St. Christopher medal on a delicate gold chain. For her life, Carmeleta would wear the medallion. During her life in times of sadness and grief she would pull from her hiding spot the letter and sit in a quiet corner of the house and reread it. In the letter it would always be summer and warm and soft.

Carmeleta felt the hands of her husband touch her shoulders and she turned and looked deeply into his eyes. He smiled at her and said nothing, but taking her by the hand he led her back into the house where the fire had gone out and must be restarted.

CHAPTER 6
THE SPEAR POINT

Majico's work around the church and home was finished now. And with the completion he had time to sit and think about his upcoming task. Already he had ridden into the garrison telling the men he would be in every Saturday for confessions and that he would always be at the church if any man needed help. Talking with the soldiers, he was not terribly impressed. Although he knew in his heart man was a violent creature, he had never really accepted that this was the only way to bring salvation to other peoples. But knowing this did not cause him confusion. All countries were the same. Kings and queens with their armies wanted power and conquest. He felt that countries used their religions as an excuse in their transgressions against other people. His country being no exception. He knew deep at the heart of the advancement into the Southwest was Spain's greed for gold and silver, not the redemption of souls. But Majico also knew that no matter what country he would have been born in, no matter what the situation, he would still have been sent by God out into the world to save souls. What mattered to Majico was what he felt in his own heart, and he knew his own heart very well.

Majico had spent many afternoons recently walking around the Indian pueblo. Each time he went, the excitment grew in him. The Indians seemed to be happy, decent lot on the whole. Although signs of alcohol abuse were many, this did not distress him greatly. He had not as of yet approached the chief or the elders, wanting to know more about the people before he spoke with the leaders. He did not want to talk with the driving force of the pueblo before he was well-versed in the everyday activities of the people.

One thing that did confuse Majico was the seeming way the pueblo ran well. There was no court system. No jails. There were little if any restrictions put on the people by their leaders. There was no written law. When Majico was first notified he would go to the new world and be sent out into the wilderness, he pictured in his mind what the heathens would be like. He figured they would be naked men with paint all over their bodies. They would be dirty and barely able to speak except with gestures and grunts. But here he found this not to be true at all. These people had a culture. They had art and games. They were clean and self-disciplined. They cooked their food and stored food for the winter. They grew crops and hunted. They married and had children. In many ways they were far superior to his own people. They did not seem to be as greedy as the Spanish. They did not covet gold or silver. And all things in life to them had a spirit. They did not own mere possessions for the sake of owning possessions like his people. And they were not divided into classes by wealth. Everybody seemed to live the same. It was a communal life. True, the medicine men and the chiefs did not work as the others, but they also did not parade around looking superior or treating the people in any way different.

One morning Majico saddled his horse and taking with him enough provisions for a day and a night, he rode towards a stretch of mountains north of his church. Majico liked riding out into the country. It gave him time to think and be close with his God. Riding as always, Majico was drawn into the expanse of the land. Not lonely with the great distance around him, he was filled with God's wonder, and he rode looking at the ageless cedar trees and the gnarled and twisted pinon trees. Around him darted jack rabbits and an occasional cottontail. It seemed the longer Majico was in the dry arid land, the more life he found around him. Majico rode quickly, wanting to reach the mountains before dark.

As dusk approached, Majico stopped his horse in front of a small opening into the mountains that led into a box canyon. He felt a chill come into his body and for a brief moment he felt like crying. Dismounting he stood motionless as waves of deep feelings and sadness came over him. Walking slowly into the mouth of the box canyon he felt as though he had been there before, and deep inside himself he knew that in time past some great happening to man had occurred there.

At the back of the canyon surrounded by sheer cliff's he discovered a small spring. In time past much larger, but still filled with sweet cool water. Drinking deeply he let his horse drink and then turned her out to eat for the night. He undid his belongings and sat down on the ground as the darkness came around him. Later by the fire he felt as though he was surrounded by hundreds of peering eyes that bore into his back. In the morning after a night of very little rest, he walked around the canyon. Scattered everywhere were fragments of broken pots and amongst the pots were many arrowheads of varous sizes and colors.

Several of the arrowheads he kept and put in his pocket. Then looking closer at the sides of the cliffs at the bases, he could see where rocks had been placed upon each other to make the bases for shelters. Standing by these he felt awed and time consumed. Who would come here? And with a ray of insight he knew it was fear. The canyon was filled with fear. Sometime in the past men had come here to hide.

As Majico continued walking and looking, he began to find many bones. Horse bones he knew. And he knew that whoever had been there had been forced to eat their animals to survive. With this Majico quickly caught his horse and going back to the spring, he saddled her and rode out of the canyon. Outside the canyon he took several deep breaths. The sun fell upon him and the chill left his bones. He would never again go back into the canyon.

Riding straight away from the canyon, he looked out upon the day and as he was looking, a bone sticking out of the sand caught his attention. Upon sighting the bone he knew it was the bone of a man, and he dismounted. As he stood looking at the protruding bone, he knew he must dig a deeper hole and bury the man. Kneeling he said a short prayer and then, with the aid of a stick and his hands, he began to dig a deep hole beside the bone. As he dug the sand slid away from more of the bones of the man until the twisted skeleton lay in view. Majico knew this man had died a terrible death. Bones were shattered and crushed, and for a moment he shivered, remembering the cries of his friends as the Indians killed them.

Moving the bones one by one into the hole he had completed, Majico could not help but see himself in time lying bleached and white under the ground, and for a brief instant life seemed shallow and useless. Everything for nothing. Just the future and the earth. For that instant it was as though God had forsaken the priest.

As Majico moved the bones he noticed a small black shiny point sticking out from the sand, and he brushed away at the object and there resting with the bones was the most magnificent spear point he had ever seen. It was over six inches long and shone like a black diamond. Majico picked the point up with two hands and looked at the deep luster. He turned it in his hands and looked through the hole that had been drilled into its base. Examining it more closely he marveled at the tiny chip marks that made the edge. And holding it he knew this point had not been made to kill but had been made with love. This point had been labored over and thought over. It had been made by a man alone filled with deep feelings and emotions, and standing with the bones and the cedar trees and the sand Majico was swept with the thoughts of Carmeleta. The feeling so strong, without thinking he placed the point over his heart and spoke, "My love, my love, gladly I would have left the church to be yours." And kneeling, his eyes closed, Majico saw a vision . . .

There was an Indian brave, young and powerful. His heart was pure and clean and his mind was alive with youth. He sat looking into a small fire and he worked on the point. With small deliberate blows the fragments fell away from the shiny stone until he set the hammer down and held the point up to the stars. From the Indian's mouth came words he could not understand, but he knew they were words of love and longing. And then behind the Indian appeared the face of Carmeleta, and Majico's heart seemed to escape from his body as a sigh spread through his chest. "My love, my love," he murmured. "How I long for thee."

Majico opened his eyes and looked at the point. He stood, placing the point in his pocket and finished burying the man. The bones reburied, he kneeled down and making the sign of the cross spoke. "Take this man into your heart, dear God, and bless him in his sacrifice."

Getting back on his horse, Majico rode quickly back to his church. It was late at night when he arrived. The horse put up, Majico sat in his small room with the lamp on and looked at the point. It was as though the point floated in his hands. In his hands he held the heart of Carmeleta. In his hands he could feel her skin and hear her tiny heart beat into his ear as his head rested on her bosom.

Going outside into the dark Majico went to the front of his church where he had lain a walkway of red flagstone. Picking up one of the flagstone blocks, he dug a small depression and placed the spear point in it. Then he replaced the flagstone. "This is love immortal," he spoke, tamping the flagstone back into the earth with his foot. "All who enter my church will walk over this gift." Going back to his room Majico fell on his knees and he thanked God for the spear point, but even in his thanks this night he could not take from his mind the vision of Carmeleta.

In the morning Majico rose early and ate a meager breakfast of beans and corn tortillas. A strange faraway gaze was in his eyes and a deep burning in his heart. Majico could not completely take his mind away from the spear point under the flagstone walkway, or the clarity with which he had seen Carmeleta's face in his vision.

CHAPTER 7
THE CHIEF AND THE ELDERS

Giant Elk paced back and forth across the large adobe room. Scattered around the room the elders of the tribe either sat in small groups or stood. For such a difficult time the men seemed relaxed and poised. Giant Elk continued to speak. "There is rumor around the pueblo that many of the young men are gathering together and speaking of forcing the Spanish out of the land." Giant Elk looked at the mixture of the elders and looking at the tired wrinkled faces he could not help but remember when he was young and the hatred he held for the Spanish. But now with time he no longer wanted to fight. Even with this feeling he found it hard to condemn the young men as he had to. It was strange — the old would reason and the young will fight. Giant Elk gathered his thoughts and continued. thoughts and continued.

"I remember well when in your youth many of you men here and I rode out in anger to kill the Spaniards. Gathering the young and brave from all the pueblos. I can remember the days when the blood of your enemies ran from our lances and how happy we were as the buzzards picked their bones. But now more and more Spaniards appear with more guns, more horses. It is not like when we were young. There were but a few, now there are many, and I know there will be no easy victors if we rise up against them. There will only be senseless killing." Giant Elk spoke and his voice had no deep conviction, no fire but the saddened tones of wisdom and love of life.

"We must gather the young rebels into our meeting hall and talk to them. If they rise up now there will be many useless kill-ings and the might of the Spaniards and their great canon will be thrown against us. Women and children will be killed and our land will be red with our blood and filled with our sorrow." All of the old men except one nodded in agreement. Time had taught them well. If the gods were with them and the medicine strong, the Spaniards would go. It was not up to the people. What had befallen the pueblo was because the gods were offended by the tribe, and if the tribe did well in all things, then the gods would surely rise up to strike the enemy down.

Man of Many Women looked at Giant Elk and the other elders. Even as an old man Man of Many Women was handsome. He was still hard and firm, liking work and riding far more than the other elders. Around his neck he wore bear claws and around his stomach he still carried his large knife. "Have we grown so old and tired we do not see what lies ahead of us? Gods do not answer your prayers. They only help us when we help ourselves. The Spaniards are not going to leave this land. They are here for our deaths and the deaths of our children and their children's children. And the longer we sit and talk and do nothing, the stronger they get. We must gather the youth to us and make them our allies, not our enemies. We must unite the people in the common cause to rid our land forever of the brown people. We must send out our warriors to raid the supply routes and make quick but steady attacks on the Spaniards. We must harrass them and make them constantly be on the alert. We must not rest in our quest but act quickly or the time will come when the Spaniards are too strong for us. And then surely they will be here forever."

Man of Many Women looked at Giant Elk. "Giant Elk, you have been closer to me than my brother. We have ridden together and fought the Spaniards. We have given many coup and danced in our war dance. We have seen great joy and great sadness in our lives and deep in your heart you know what I say is the truth. We must all remember the younger days of our lives. We must rise and fight and give our land back to our children. The Spaniards put laws upon us: We must not gather and talk war against the Spaniards. We must give them food and material. And now their religious men come and we must listen to them. They whip people who dissent. They bring alcohol to our people and make spies within our midst. We are not sheep to be herded into corners and slowly slaughtered." Man of Many Women looked at the men in the room, but he could tell his words were unheard. He spun on his heel and walked to the door. "You are women," he spat, and left the room.

The door hanging open, Giant Elk looked at the open door and scanned the men in the room. Truly, he thought to himself, we are like women. Too content in our comfort and old age to see what harm we bring to our people. The other men moved nervously looking at each other for encouragement.

Giant Elk cleared his throat. "Listen. Find out who the dissenters are and get word to me. I wish to speak with the men, but I do not wish for them to be afraid. If the gods wish for them to war, then there is nothing we can do but sit and pray for the best."

The old men filed from the meeting room. Giant Elk stayed long after the others had left and moved slowly around the room. Many years ago when he was a boy his father had told him of a strange dream a medicine man of old had had. A dream telling of a strange crisscross across the land and small homes with people around the homes being brown and white and yellow. It was strange to think of these things after so many years. Memories not thought of when one was a youth.

Giant Elk shook his head. It was just an old dream, a dream in fragments now. Lost with the medicine man years ago when he died. It was different with the Spaniards. They had books with markings that told of many ancient things. Books to bring back the memories and pass on wisdom of the ages. Giant Elk felt a shiver run through his body, and deep within himself he knew his people were doomed. It was only time now.

But what worried Giant Elk the most was not the soldiers but the strange little round man who was coming to see him tomorrow. The priest. Here was the true enemy of the people. Here was the man that would strip away from them their gods and beliefs. Here was a man who would preach of one god. Of a mean vengeful god. A god of the stars and heavens. Not a god of the trees and land. Not a god of summer and winter, spring and fall. Here was a man who would take the youth away from the people. Who would tell the people the dances and ceremonies were evil.

Giant Elk stood and ran his hands over his long white flowing hair. It seemed there was no peace in life, only fragments of time when all was restful. Moments of time in the arms of a lover. Moments of time watching a child at play. But around these tiny moments was chaos and grief for man. A struggle, a constant struggle. Giant Elk shrugged his drooping shoulders and took a deep breath. Dinner would be ready soon. He walked from the meeting room out into the fading day. Already the western horizon turned crimson. After dinner he must think. He must be ready for this man of God from the church. He must not falter. There must be a way to make his people strong even with the statement from the Spanish captain that all Indians must attend the masses the priest would give at the pueblo.

Man of Many Women sat and puffed thoughtfully on his pipe. He had sent his woman from the house to be with her sister. If she had stayed he could not have thought. Women had always been bad for thinking. After eleven wives he knew women were good for cooking, washing, and sleeping with. Besides this he had never found another good quality in one. They were noisy, talked too much and expected far too much from a man. He firmly believed if they didn't have a love nest, they should be fed to the dogs.

Man of Many Women was in a grim mood. After leaving the meeting hall he had walked around the pueblo. It was like walking in an enemy camp. Although the people worked and talked and the children ran, there was still the feeling of the Spaniards. There was a nervousness to the pueblo. People looked over their shoulders at the shadows as if all the shadows were Spaniards. Man of Many Women sat and in his mind's eye he mapped out his plan. He knew Jagged Knife was the leader of the young braves. He also knew Jagged Knife was a strong and unafraid man, but he was lacking in planning. Jagged Knife would need a man as he; older, wiser and more patient. He must meet with Jagged Knife and tell him how to fight his battle. He knew the Spaniards grew in strength every day and he also knew it would be a long and tedious fight to drive them from the land. Man of Many Women put his pipe down and stood. He would go and get his wife now and bring her back. Of all his women there had been none like her. Wrapped in her arms, one forgot all about the world and only dreamed of her skin and sighs.

Giant Elk stood outside his home and watched the night sky. For so many years the people had been here. Not far away, where the little priest slept, were the ruins of his parents' ancestors. This was a timeless land. A land where the people were meant to be. There were so many strange twists to life. Just when one thought all would be well, there was something else. But it was different at night. The dark coming in around you, bringing rest and hope. Each night was a promise of a new day. And with each new day one never knew what would happen to add to the history of life. Giant Elk took one last look at the stars and walked back into his home. Tonight he wished he was as Man of Many Women and had a young warm maiden to be in his bed. Even if he could do nothing, she would be young and firm and a pleasure to be with.

CHAPTER 8
MAJICO AND THE CHIEF

Majico sat and looked around the bare room. The walls had been whitewashed and besides the small rug he sat on there was nothing else in the room except a round fireplace in the corner. It was a comfortable room and had the feel of many deep conversations and a cool almost holy feel to it. He had been led here silently by two old Indians. Men who looked at him indifferently but not menacingly. They had opened the door and he had entered and they had shut the door without speaking. The captain had told him the chief spoke excellent Spanish and this made Majico wish he could speak Indian. He must learn the language if he was to get the trust of the Indians. Giant Elk entered the room and looked at the priest. Majico stood and as the chief neared he held out his hand to shake. Both men shook hands firmly and the chief sat down on the rug, pointing next to him to part of the rug. "Sit here," he spoke. "To talk as we, we must be close." Majico sat down beside the chief and looked deep into the dark eyes surrounded by the furrowed skin. Giant Elk was a proud and strong looking man, but deep within his eyes was the look of a man defeated. Giant Elk in turn gazed at the priest and he could not help but smile looking at the plump round little man.

Giant Elk spoke first. "You Spaniards are a strange lot." Majico laughed, much to the surprise of Giant Elk. "Man is a strange lot, my friend," Majico answered. "All of us are men, all of us are strange."

Giant Elk smiled and felt a tinge of hope in his heart. Maybe this man would be different, maybe this man would understand. "Before you came," Giant Elk continued, "our people were the only people for many many miles. But now you have come and with your coming you have brought confusion and fear to my people. Where once we ruled, now we are ruled. Where once we were the only ones, now we are together. And you and I must decide how we can live together and not destroy each other."

Majico listened to Giant Elk and a great respect for the man entered his body. Giant Elk rose from the rug and began to walk around the room. "My friend, we are a different people than your people. I have asked many men about your god. And I know your god is not our god. We have many gods and our gods are the hearts of our people. Why must we come to yours? Why must the captain tell us we must attend your mass?"

Majico looked at Giant Elk and he grew angry. "I told no one to order you to attend my mass. I will speak to the captain about this." Majico was angered. There would be no force used in his preaching. The people would come over with free will and love. God was truth and hope. Man did not learn through laws but by choice.

Giant Giant Elk looked at Majico and saw the flush on his face and spoke, "I am happy to hear such words." Giant Elk turned and spoke with his back to Majico. "When I was a boy, your people were here. They were greedy bad people. They came looking for cities of gold and silver. They took our women and forced our people to work. In time we could take this no longer, and we rose up against your people and priests like you, and both of our peoples lost many men. But now I am an old man. Old and tired, and I do not wish to fight." And then turning he looked at Majico, "We must decide how we can live together. We must decide how my people can stay as their own people and your people can search for their gold and silver until they once again wish to go home."

Majico looked at the old chief and a great feeling of sadness came over him. This man was not a savage, he was not a heathen. He had gods and hope and love. He was no different from Majico. And for the first time Majico knew he would be in this land his entire life. For the first time Majico saw God's plan for him. He would never see Spain again. He would see nothing but the land around his little church and deep in his heart Majico knew that above all things not he nor God had the right to take away the hearts of any people. All gods were the one God. God in his wisdom made himself into many things so that all people in his world would come to believe in him. Majico stood and looked at the chief. "Your gods are my God. They are just the manifestation of his great wisdom and love."

Giant Elk walked towards the little priest and gripped him by the arms. "Priest, you do not know how your words make me feel. Surely with you we will find the answers we seek."

That night Majico stayed at the pueblo and ate with the chief. He marveled at the women as they cooked and for a moment he thought of his little room by the church and a great wave of sadness spread over him. He ate the dried meat and cooked corn with relish and smiled at the ladies as they laughed watching the priest eat. Giant Elk after eating took out his pipe and lit it. Taking several puffs he handed it to Majico. Majico took a deep puff and coughed loudly and said, "I don't smoke." Giant Elk grinned. "If you live in this land for long, you will smoke, my friend. The desert will make you smoke."

Majico, his head spinning, felt giddy but did not answer. That night lying on several elk hides in a small room, Majico looked into the darkened ceiling. He would keep his church open but he would force no Indian to attend. In time one Indian would come and then others and then others and slowly with love and good works he would get his converts. But he would always let the people remain Indians. They were special people. A people in their way close to God. Majico lay and sleep came over him peacefully.

In the morning after drinking mint tea he shook hands with Giant Elk. "Come and visit me, Giant Elk," he spoke. "We are friends in all things. And if you need help come, I am good with the sick." After leaving the pueblo Majico went directly to the captain's headquarters.

"Captain," he spoke sternly entering the building. The captain felt sick and thought, O my God, it has started. "There will be no orders for the Indians to attend my church, do you understand?"

The captain at a loss for words nodded his head in agreement. Majico turned on his heel and stepped briskly to his horse. Riding out it was a glorious day. A day when one should be sitting and looking at the world and finding peace within oneself.

CHAPTER 9

MAN OF MANY WOMEN
AND JAGGED KNIFE

Jagged Knife had ridden for many days and visted all the pueblos for over 100 miles. At each pueblo he gathered around him the young and filled their hearts with fire for the Spaniards. Many of the pueblos were ruled more severely than his. There were stories of beatings and many hangings. And there were stories of many rapes of the women. There were also stories of men rounded up a put in chains and forced to work the mines for the Spaniard's gold and silver. With each day Jagged Knife's heart became heavier and heavier and his mind ached for the death of the Spanish. But although Jagged Knife knew he could lead the people, he knew he needed help. Help from someone who he did not know. Help to plan and make sure the plans were executed well.

Riding back towards his own pueblo, Jagged Knife made camp several miles away from the pueblo. Here tucked safely in the back of a box canyon by a tiny spring, he stayed. Only a few of the braves knew of his hiding place. There were myths about this canyon in the pueblo. Stories how in many years past the canyon had been the refuge for the people and how during one great battle when the people were starving and about to be defeated, the gods sent out into the enemy a spirit that killed the chief of the invaders and sent them running back out of the land of the people. Jagged Knife did not know if he believed in the myth but always in the canyon he felt safe and protected. There were many broken pots in the canyon and horse bones, but to Jagged Knife there was no sense of history or time. There was only today and tomorrow and his burning desire to rid his people of the Spaniards.

Riding towards the canyon he had passed the Spaniard's man of God's church and home. There was nobody there and he had gone into the church. Inside it was a strange place. He did not know what the altar was or the cedar branches over it. But to his surprise the room had a warm feeling even in the coolness of the adobe. Leaving the church he had gone to the small one-room house behind the church and inside he was amazed at the simplicity of the room. There was only a small bed, a washstand and a thing that was not a chair which he did not know was a praying stand. There was a book which he thumbed through, but had no comprehension of what it was. Back outside he mounted his horse quickly and rode towards the canyon. It was a strange man who would wish to be alone. Did not this Spanish man of God long for the companionship of women? Did he not like the sound of children or life around him? Was he so devoted to his God that there could be no joy in his life? Truly the Spaniards had a strange God.

Leaving the area, Jagged Knife looked all around him. There to his left was the long sand and clay hill stretching down from the mesa top he and his friends as children would run and jump and slide down. Back to his rear was the evil peak, sticking out into the horizon like a table. Even with his strength Jagged Knife had never ventured there. He had been close before but had skirted his horse around the point. Many of his friends had been there and came back telling tales of strange figures on the rock and of a horse that seemed to breathe and run as if alive carved in the stone. But within a few weeks it seemed the people who went to the cliff always came down with bad luck. A prized horse would die. Coyotes would get their turkeys. And although Jagged Knife was not superstitious, he could not see tempting the gods either.

Jagged Knife sat around a small fire. Around him not a sound penetrated the canyon. The fire dancing before him, the burning in his heart, slowly went away as he thought about his first raid on the Spanish. The cut on his face would forever tell the people he was not a coward — would tell them he was forever willing to die for his people. The raid had been several years before at a time the Spaniards called Christmas. A time of rest and prayers for the Spaniards. They had taken their ponies and ridden north to a settlement called Santa Fe. Here the Spaniards stocked their gold and silver and other trade goods for shipment back to Mexico. They had tethered the ponies outside of town and with the dark rushed in. In a wild charge, yelping and singing their war cries, they fell upon the sleeping soldiers and killed many. They set buildings on fire and killed many horses and mules. One Spaniard had been on guard duty and with a swift stroke of his knife had barely missed cutting Jagged Knife's throat but the point only lay open his cheek. Jagged Knife had buried his knife into the heart of the man and stood twisting it, watching the man's eyes bulge out and feeling the warm sticky blood cover his hand. Jagged Knife would forever remember this killing. How his hate flowed out through his knife point and how the Spaniard died slowly in much pain.

Jagged Knife, hearing a noise in the canyon, stood quickly and walked away from his fire. Now he could hear the approaching footsteps of one man. Jagged Knife drew his knife from his belt and crouched deeper into the shadows. He watched as the lone figure approached and a voice cut the air. "It is I, Man of Many Women. I come to talk." Jagged Knife stepped out of the shadows but before putting away his knife he made sure it was Man of Many Women. Putting the knife away, Jagged Knife stepped up to the fire. "Sit," he motioned. "I was about to cook some rabbit, are you hungry?" Man of Many Women laughed. "I am always hungry," and he sat down.

As the rabbit cooked, Man of Many Women filled his pipe and smoked. Sitting with Jagged Knife he felt old looking at the lean strong body of the young man. Time was not kind to any man.

Eating, Jagged Knife spoke. "What brings you to my camp, and how did you know where I was?"

Man of Many Women smiled. "Young men are not good at keeping secrets, my friend," he answered. "It does not take long to know what goes on in a small pueblo like ours." Then swallowing the bite of rabbit, he continued. "I have come to help you. I, too, want to drive the Spaniards from the land. I am tired of the elders doing nothing, letting our people be trampled and used." He looked out into the dark. "This land is our land, given to us by our gods. We have been here forever. Everywhere is history of our past. There are the markings on the rocks, the broken pots and arrow points. The bones of horses and mules. The old ruins of tribes past. In all these things we are and in time our ruins will be reminders to our children that we are forever a part of this land. It is time for the war dance, time to rise up and drive the enemy of the people from our land and you and your followers need me. For as you are strong and young, I am older and cunning."

Jagged Knife looked at the old warrior and smiled. Here was the answer. Here was the completion of the circle that would bring him and his men to victory.

Man of Many Women refilled is pipe. The pipe lit, he talked solemnly. "We must never forget the power of the Spanish. They are a strong and greedy people. We must be like the snake crawling on our bellies to harrass and raid his camps. We must attack his shipment lines, cutting him off from his world to the south. But our attacks must be relentless. We must not take prisoners or spoils. We must kill and destroy. And we must be fast. Never in the same place for long. Always moving. You must go to the pueblos and gather all your men. In one month's time we will meet here. Then we will divide the braves into groups and send each group out to specific tasks, picking each time another place for us to meet. We can never gather in the same place twice. And we must also be wary of spies within the pueblos. The weak ones who would deceive their own people for the blackness in their heart."

In the morning Man of Many Women rode back to the pueblo and Jagged Knife rode out onto the land to go once more to the other pueblos, but this time to bring the warriors with him. As he rode he could hear the war songs and feel in his chest the beat of the drums. "It is my calling," he spoke to the sky as he kicked his horse and galloped out into the vastness around him.

CHAPTER 10
THE CAPTAIN PREPARES

Captain Aguirre was distressed. Over the past weeks there had been more and more rumors circulating about the unrest of the Indians. He had been summoned to Santa Fe the previous week to a general meeting of detachment commanders concerning the rumor there were many young braves ready to rise up and strike against the scattered garrisons. The captain knew what could happen if all the pueblos banded together. There would be no way the Spanish could hold out. There was much trouble in Mexico now. Supplies were slow in coming into the settlements and the chancellor and his subordinates were constantly at each other's throats over the gold and silver that came back to Mexico. Many of the garrison commanders in the area secretly hoarded gold for themselves, causing much unrest and jealousy. All the men had been put on the alert, but that would be no help if the Indians truly wished to fight. For the captain it was strange. He knew how the Indians felt. He knew that if he was in Spain and people invaded his land, he would rather die. Now after the years in the wilderness he only wished to be home. Not hear worrying about dying or making sure gold got back to the rich coffers of Spain. If one thing was going right for the captain, it was the way the priest, Majico, stayed out of his way.

It was good to have a priest that was not over-zealous. Already over the past months many Indians attended the priest's church by their own will and he had seen several Indians wearing rough wood carved crucifixes the priest worked on daily. The captain figured the Indians decided if there was another god, it could not hurt to follow him also. He had only seen Majico in passing over the last weeks. Majico spent more and more time with the chief and the elders. At times the captain wished to know what they talked about, but the priest would not confide this information. All Majico would say when questioned was, "God is not only a Spaniard."

Through many spies the captain had discovered Jagged Knife was the leader of the young braves. But he could not find Jagged Knife. If he could, he would have the brave locked up. But he had also heard there were many older braves now joining the growing numbers of young braves. This worried him as it would give the young radicals people with age and wisdom, not just feeling. He had heard the stories of the first Spaniards in the area and how the Indians had risen up and driven them out. The Spaniards who returned to Mexico told tales of men staked out on ant holes and covered with honey until the ants devoured them slowly. They told stories of men tied to stakes who were slowly skinned until they died. There was talk of men caught and their stomachs slit until their insides fell out on the ground, and then dogs allowed to eat their intestines while they still lived.

The stories made the captain pale and afraid. At first the Indians had welcomed them into the area. But it was hard to control soldiers far away from home. One incident led to another and soon force had to be used against the Indians and then rules set up and then shortsighted men put the Indians to work. God, the captain wished he was back in Spain. He would love to see a beautiful perfumed Spanish lady. There was not enough gold in this God-forsaken land to keep him here. Captain Aguirre sat down at his desk and picked up a sheet of paper. Reading it slowly once again he knew that this would set the stage for the battle to come. It was an order from the King of Spain granting large areas of land to various people in the territory. The land would go to a Mr. Ortiz — 280,000 acres. Mr. Ortiz was a wealthy trader now living in Santa Fe who had married his young daughter off to a diplomat close to the king. She had been escorted to Mexico and then taken to Spain. In return, Mr. Ortiz was given this land. The Indians would learn of this soon when Ortiz and his men would be in the area. The captain had learned Ortiz was hiring many men and would soon come out and build a large hacienda and start to run sheep. The captain knew this would be the blow that would send the Indians against the Spaniards. Now they would be told the land that had been theirs for generations was given to other people by a person and country they did not even know.

Rising from his desk the captain walked wearily out into the day. Looking towards the Indian pueblo he smiled faintly, knowing in his heart he would die in this dry forsaken land.

CHAPTER 11
THE END

Over the next several years Jagged Knife along with Man of Many Women wreaked havoc on the Spaniards. They raided the supply routes and small outposts at will, never staying in one place very long. The Spaniards were on constant patrol. But when they were on patrol their garrisons would be undermanned and the garrisons would be raided. The Indians took no prisoners, killing all that were in their way. Captain Aguirre was killed one fall day, stepping from his office. An arrow shot from an unseen Indian pierced his heart. His body was buried and time removed the marker.

Jagged Knife led many raids and became known for his courage and ruthlessness. He died one late afternoon galloping his horse towards a Spanish patrol when the horse fell and Jagged Knife broke his neck. The Spaniards who found him, knowing who he was by the scar on his face, took him to Santa Fe and propped him up against the courthouse for all to see. He stayed propped up and covered with lime for several weeks until one night somebody stole his body and he was forever put to rest. Man of Many Women lived many years, dying in his sleep with the Spaniards still in control of his people.

Majico would bring many converts into the church. He was liked by the Indians and became a mediator between the soldiers and the Indians. He never forced any man into his god. He was killed by three young braves from a distant pueblo one sunny afternoon. He had been in his church praying when he heard horses and coming out his chest had been filled wth arrows. Falling on the flagstone walkway to the church, his chest fell across the flagstone with the spear point buried underneath, and his life's blood covered the stone and settled into the brown clay soil of the earth.

When Carmeleta was fifty-two years old, she would receive word of Majico's death years earlier. With tears streaming down her face, she went to a quiet spot outside of town where there was a little pond with frogs and birds and bees, and she sat until the dark remembering the round priest and his smile and the goodness of his heart. She would live to be ninety-seven years old, outliving her husband and children, and die a woman blessed by God.

Across the land the seasons came and went. The Indian abandoned his old pueblos and moved to several large pueblos in different areas of the territory. The small adobe church fell to ruin beside the ancient Indian ruin, and the abandoned pueblo crumbled to return to the earth. The Spanish garrison was erased from the memory of the land and replaced by Don Ortiz's sprawling hacienda. Devil's Peak withstood time and weather and the pictographs remained as if made yesterday. The horse still flew with the wind and seemed as though alive. And out of Mexico came the Mexicans. Poor, ignorant people looking for a new life, carrying with them the new God of the Catholic and looking for redemption and hope in a virgin land.

Santa Fe became the capital of the territory. Filled with

soldiers from Spain and traders from all over the country. It was a blend of white man, Indian and Mexican and the children of all three races.

And once again the land did not care or feel, remember or need. It only was what it was, the immortal land. Tying in all history with the scars it carried on its soil and rocks.

BOOK THREE
THE MEXICANS

CHAPTER 1
THE RICH AND THE POOR — 1835 A.D.

Don Ortiz was a powerful man. A man whose father years earlier had been given over 280,000 acres by the King of Spain. This land his father had bequeathed to him and with it the power and fortune it brought. To the mountains on the western side of the land, the Ortiz gold mine brought out of the earth high grade gold and silver. From the mountains to the east, sheep and cattle grew fat. And in the flats between the mountains, these same sheep and cattle lived out the cold months. Ortiz himself lived in a rambling adobe house that was built over the ruins of an old Spanish garrison and next to a crumbling pueblo. Here surrounded by cottonwood trees, the house was cool in the summer and warm in the winter. Ortiz had a lovely wife and three children. He also had his pick of the women in town, changing mistresses at will.

He was a man born to power and comfort and a man who needed more. All his wishes were carried out, all his desires fulfilled. To control his sprawling empire he hired over thirty men who would kill at the drop of a hat. These men he paid well for their dirty work. Also on his land he let live several Mexican families who took care of his sheep and cattle in return for the right to have a small garden and run a few sheep and goats of their own. These people bought food from his store at his headquarters and cloth for their clothes. They were a poor simple people. People who knew they would never be rich and powerful. A passionate people who lived with the land and prayed to their Virgin Mary. To Ortiz they were peons, no better than dogs. People with no backbone or desire to own more than they had. Not knowing the comfort of a nice home or the sweet touch of delicate perfumed women. And Ortiz treated them as such — dogs to do his bidding. He would extend them credit at his store and then when they could not pay, he would indenture them for the rest of their lives. "It is easy," he would tell his friends, "to control the poor. They have no idea of life." And he would laugh while the rich friends around him smiled and chuckled at his remarks.

But deep inside themselves, most people hated Ortiz. Hated him for his power and his bearing. Hated him for his mistresses. And within the household of Ortiz there was little happiness. Although his children had all life could offer, money did not bring them love or comfort of the heart. And Ortiz knowing this, with all his worldly goods, was a sad and bitter man lost in his world of power.

Raymond Lujan stepped back from the house and smiled. For three weeks he and hs wife had worked from early in the morning until late at night hauling the heavy flat rocks and stacking them using mud as mortar to build the two-room home he now looked at. Across the roof he had interwoven salt cedar branches and covered them with mud. Inside he had built a large rock fireplace which would be used for both heat and cooking until he could save enough money to buy a woodstove. Sandra, his wife, walked up to him rubbing the mud from her hands. She was a short stocky woman with wide cheeks and broad lips that throughout all the hardship and toil of their lives together had never ceased to break into a smile. Raymond put his rough hand in his wife's and they stood looking at their new home. "Lovely," Sandra spoke, kissing her husband on the cheek.

"But not like the Ortiz hacienda," Raymond answered.

Sandra laughed, "Yes, but we are not Ortiz nor will we ever be."

Raymond looked into the eyes of his wife and his heart was filled with his love as it had been every day over the past four years. "It is a good day, my wife," he spoke, pulling her to his side.

Sandra giggled and pulled away from him. "I must get water for tonight and you must get wood."

Raymond looked over at the rough shelter of rocks and mud in which they had lived for the past five weeks. And looked back at the rock house. "Tonight we will make love in our home and maybe now God will bless us with children." Sandra, already walking to the small stream, wiggled her large hips. "Tonight then we must both take a bath. I do not want any stinking man on my body."

Raymond stood and looked at the house and the gently sloping hill behind it. On the top of this slope was a level mesa from where one could see out upon the land. Here many evenings he had stood with his wife looking at the ruins of the old church and Indian pueblo and at Devil's Peak. Here he had stood without his wife, yearning to have a hacienda like the Ortiz hacienda only a short distance away. Without Sandra, Raymond did not know what he would do. Before here there had been no life — only poverty. Now there was still poverty but there was life.

Raymond glanced at his wife bending over filling the large heavy water cans. My love, my love, he thought, what do you see in me? He walked over to the shelter that had been their home and picking up an axe by the door, he went out to the flats to chop wood for the evening.

Walking past the crumbling church, Raymond remembered the day they arrived at this spot. He and his wife had left Mexico on foot with four burros. On the burros were all their possessions. A few pots and pans, corn, flour and dried goat, a pick and several shovels, an axe and a small tent. There was no hope back in their little village. Only the constant raids by the bandits, and diseases. They left nothing behind. No family or people one could call friends, only bad memories.

Following the Rio Grande for weeks and weeks they saw many places they would have liked to stop but there was always the pull to go further. Somewhere over the horizon was another place. A place for them and only them. Following the Rio Grande River had not been hard, but when they came to the great expanse of rock and cactus that divided the territory, they grew despondent. After several days of hot desert walking, they almost turned their donkeys and headed back south. But they did not and continued on through the unforgiving land.

After several months they had come to the edge of the mesa. Standing there looking out across the endless land, they had seen the old church and Indian ruin. There was no roof, only four crumbling walls. Behind the church they could see what once had been a meager house. And here also was a small clear running stream with pure cool water. Sandra had looked at the furrowed brown face of her husband and spoke.

"Here, here is where we will build and live. This will be our land and our children's land."

"But there is land nicer than this," Raymond had protested.

"There is always something nicer," his wife countered. And Raymond knew he was bettered and this would be the spot they would settle.

Moving into a small cave in the side of the slope, they mortared the front and spent time resting. It was good to be in one spot and not moving. On the third week they woke up one morning to find themselves confronted by six men. Men with guns and lassos riding fine horses.

"What are you doing here?" one spoke, not unfriendly but not

96

friendly either.

Raymond looked at the men. "This is going to be my home."

Another of the men laughed grimly. "First, my friend, we must go talk to Mr. Ortiz. He owns all of this land."

Following the men with their fine horses on his burro, Raymond felt as though his world had come to an end. After so many miles he had settled on another man's land.

The first time Raymond rode into the Ortiz hacienda, he could not comprehend all that was around him. There were stables and many houses. There was a store and a livery and a large smoke house. Everywhere were children and dogs. Out behind were goats and sheep and turkeys. And there was the Ortiz house. Rambling, larger than any house Raymond had ever seen. Each room with its own fireplace. Completely surrounding the house was a large porch and sitting on the porch in fine clothes and handmade boots with silver spurs was Don Ortiz.

"Another squatter," one of the men spoke, pointing at Raymond.

Don Ortiz stood and looked at the square-shouldered Mexican. "Did you kow this is my land?" he spoke gruffly.

Raymond shook his head, "No, sir, I did not know."

"Well, then that is good. If you are to stay, you must work for me one day out of the week. Of all the sheep and goats you own each year, when they produce young, you will give me one quarter of your yield. In turn, in ten years I will give you 100 acres of the land."

Raymond felt relief spread throughout his body and he nodded hs head in amazement at the generous offer. Riding back to his home, Raymond was exhilarated. Land, he would have land. Land for all time.

Sitting back down on his proch, Mr. Ortiz laughed to hmself. Dumb Mexicans, they came here looking for hope. Did they not know there was no hope? In ten years — if he managed to survive that long on this inhospitable land — then Ortiz would have him killed. He would never give up his property to any man. There were over ten families like this new man. All living scattered over the expanse of his domain. All dreaming of the day they would have their hundred acres. Ortiz sipped a cool glass of water and looked at the slowly disappearing image of the Mexican.

Raymond began chopping the dead cedar tree. His axe taking clean bites with each swing. Tonight his wife was making a chicken and tonight, after a bath, he would lay within her arms. Life was good, life was very good.

Returning with the wood Raymond saw Sandra sitting in the small pool they had dug away from the stream for bathing. She did not see him and he stood breathing shallowly as though the sound of his breathing would make his wife notice him. She was not a pretty women by any means, but she was a true woman. And he loved her deeply.

Raymond lay the blanket over the straw-filled mattress. The dim flicker of a burning candle danced along the sides of the walls. Sitting on a stool in front of the fire, his wife brushed her long black hair. He loved her hair. More than her breasts or thighs, he loved her long flowing hair. Running his fingers through her hair was like a rosary, slowly taking all bitterness from his body. He removed his clothes. The bath had made him feel fresh and alive. Sandra stood by the fire and removed her dress. Raymond watched as her round body came into view. Sandra had round full shoulders and large breasts that at twenty-five already sagged. Her hips were large and square and her legs muscled and stocky. Raymond loved every bit of the woman. Beauty to him was truly on the inside. He would remember always his grandfather's words when he was a boy and did not understand what his grandfather spoke. "Raymond," he would say, "When you marry, marry yourself a strong woman who is a little fat," and his grandfather would smile. "Because as you get old, the softer you will like them." Now Raymond understood completely. Sandra's skin was soft. It fell over him like a warm blanket. Her body was like the earth, he could mold and shape her skin into his dreams.

Sandra walked to the bed and smiling lay down beside Raymond. Raymond slid his rough and calloused hand gently over her large breast and looked into her eyes. "Sandra, my love, we have a home and we have hope."

Outside the small cozy two-room rock house a slight breeze circled over the land. It passed over a box canyon and slid gracefully down into plains and around Devil's Peak then circled and swept over the Ortiz hacienda. As it neared Raymond and Sandra's house, it seemed to die and sit waiting, listening to the sounds of the lovers.

CHAPTER 2
THE PROBLEM

Don Ortiz walked briskly back and forth across the sparsely furnished room. There was only a large table with twelve chairs and a fireplace in the room. Standing and sitting around the room were ten men. Some smoking fine cigars, some sipping brandy. But they were all distressed. Rumor had come from the Spanish governor in Santa Fe that there were reports the United States would soon invade this land. Now over the years Spain had forgotton about this part of the world. The government wracked by greed and corruption and constant war, she could no longer afford to worry about this small distant possession. There were only eighty-five soldiers in the garrison at Santa Fe. The Pueblo Indians had not been a problem in over seventy-five years. But now if the United States would march into the area, there was nothing to stop them. They would take the land and with this the large land owners would lose their power and fortunes.

Manuel Lujan sipped his brandy and looked at Don Ortiz. "We must send an envoy to Mexico City and tell the Chancellor we need men and weapons. For over 150 years our families have controlled this land. We have fought off the Indians, many of our people have died. This is our land now. They will send help.

Ortiz looked at the man disapprovingly. "This is not true. The Chancellor will not send soldiers. He has enough problems of his own wondering where to hide his gold."

With this Ortiz laughed a sarcastic laugh. "I feel what we must do is make contact with the government of the United States, telling them we welcome their troops and government and we will join their flag. Then they might let us keep our property."

The men in the room looked at each other and knew this was the only way. They were defenseless against invasion. They must change alliances as all men of power had done throughout history. It was not a matter of pride, it was simply a matter of common sense. These men in their comfort were not proud enough to fight. A life of leisure and fine women made a man soft and complacent.

Don Ortiz spoke again, "It is imperative we send men we trust. The governor in Santa Fe must not get word of what we do. It could be called treason and then Spain would take away our land."

For several hours more the men talked and it was decided that

Don Ortiz's son Henrico and Orlando Escavars would go to the Oklahoma territory and approach the United States government there to send their written document to the President.

The men gone, Don Ortiz sat alone in the large room. Inside himself his hatred for the Spanish government festered. Did they not know of the work and hardships his ancestors had gone through to hold this land? Did they not remember the bloody Indian uprisings and the years of killing and fear? Did they not appreciate the gold and silver pouring out of the land into the rich coffers of Spain? Don Ortiz had been born on this land. His father's father had been born in Spain and came here for the glory of Spain. He had been killed by raiding Comanches on this land. Behind the hacienda surrounded by a high rock wall were eight of the Don Ortiz family laid to rest on this land.

Rising slowly Ortiz mumbled to himself, "It is like all things, when life is good, every man is behind you, but when life is bad, the rats flee from the ship." He walked down the long hall of the house. Passing his wife's bedroom door he stopped for a moment, but then continued to walk. "Daughter of a whore," he spat. But as he walked to his room, he could not quell the sad feeling that came into his heart as he thought of his wife and the softness he had found in her body years earlier. If he had not been such a fool and been caught sleeping with Consuelo he could still be sleeping with his wife. Ever since the other woman there had been many more, and he knew he and his wife would never be the same again.

Don Ortiz sat down on his bed and removed his tall black boots. Around him he could feel his empire crumbling and for the first time in his life, he felt defenseless as any other mortal man.

Isabella Ortiz sat in front of a large mirror and brushed her long blue-black silky hair. At forty-three she was still a striking woman. Unlike most Spanish women, she was still thin. From the flow of her cheeks to the grace of her long thin fingers, her body was as a river. Each part of her melted into the other. She had heard her husband walk by the room and hesitate, and then continue. And for a moment her heart had fluttered, wanting to stand and unbolt the door and call to him, but she did not, could not. Isabella set the brush down and walked to her bed. Taking off her robe she lay down and took the bible from the stand beside the bed.

Life had been so happy years earlier. She was sixteen when she first saw Don Ortiz. Her father owned a small inn and restaurant in Santa Fe. They were not rich, but they were also not poor. Her parents were very happy people who loved to dance and sing. During every holiday people came for miles to be at the inn for the parties and good food. There were many different people. All hardworking people who left the inn happy and warm inside. Isabella was sweeping the porch to the inn when Ortiz had ridden by one afternoon. Her young heart fluttered in her chest and her eyes bore into the sight of the young man. He rode a huge black horse, wellgroomed and shiny. His saddle shone with silver and leather work and his boots were as black as the horse. His clothes clung to his body like skin, and his back was straight as his gaze seemed to sweep over the heads of the people around him. Asking about the man, she found out he was the son of Marcus Ortiz. The biggest land owner in the area. He was by far the richest man between here and Mexico. It was not for six months that Ortiz noticed the girl, but when he did, he was struck and three months later they were married.

For the first year Isabella had never been so happy. Each day he gave her a new dress. Each week there were grand parties to attend with the important people of Santa Fe. At night their love making brought her into great worlds of ecstasy. His hands upon her were like coals. His kisses made her cry out with passion. Their bodies merged into one was though they had truly been created together.

When Isabella was eighteen, she had her first child. A beautiful baby girl with dancing eyes like her mother. Ortiz could not hide his disappointment. When she was twenty, she had her second child, another lovely daughter, and slowly Isabella felt her husband's love slipping away. She would do everything for him, but many nights he would ride into town from the hacienda and not return for days.

When Isabella was twenty-two, she had her third child, a strong baby boy, and once again it seemed her husband loved her dearly. But soon she came to know his love was only for the boy, and she and her two daughters were segregated. Outwardly there was no change in Isabella. She was still the charming hostess. Still the lovely wife. Running the household. Keeping peace with the cooks and housekeepers. But inwardly Isabella grew hard and sheltered. Making love to her husband was a duty, not a pleasure, and the love that had been in her heart though still love, was a love only of memory.

When Isabella was twenty-six, she had her fourth child. Another boy, but he had died from the fever within a month. And during her grief, her husband had once again ridden into town many nights. It was then through ladies she knew in town that she heard about her husband's transgression with many women, and it was then she would forever withhold herself from Ortiz. She would forever be the dutiful Catholic wife, but she would not nor could not ever forgive her husband. As their years together progressed, there was very little communication between them and the household became silent and cloudy.

Isabella opened her Bible and began to read, while down the hall her husband slept.

CHAPTER 3
LABOR LOST

Sandra watched her husband ride off on the burro towards the Ortiz hacienda. Once a week he would go to do his agreed day of work. They were hard days for Raymond. He would clean stalls or dig fence posts, cut wood or whatever menial task needed doing. Over the past months Raymond had met the other Mexicans like himself living on the Ortiz land. They had told him Ortiz was not a man to be trusted, but Raymond had never divulged this to his wife. His wife lived in the dream of owning ther own land. But with each passing month, as Raymond's bill at the Ortiz store grew larger, he became more and more despondent. There was no way the amount of sheep or goats he possessed could bring enough money to pay his bill. And now that Sandra was pregnant, there would be more mouths to feed and more bills.

Raymond was not a complicated man, not a learned man. He could neither read nor write. But as time passed, he began to feel cheated by Ortiz. He knew the prices at the store were high, but what could he do? He knew one day a week working for Ortiz robbed him from his own tasks and he wondered how some men seem to have so much and some so very little. But in Raymond's mind there was no way out of the trap. If he had been religious like his wife, he could believe in salvation, but Raymond had never been religious. He did not know if he believed in God or not although he did go to church when the priest came from Santa Fe to the Ortiz ranch. He did this only for the sake of his wife.

What bothered Raymond the most was the way his wife had to

live. They had a small wooden bed, several hand-hewn wooden tables, and two kerosene lamps. Sandra possessed only three dresses and several warm coats. Working at the Ortiz hacienda, he had seen the women of the household many times. He would see them with their fine dresses and jewelry and he would think of his poor wife working long hours each day, feeding the chickens and pigs and burros. Walking out into the land to fetch wood and water, sitting in their crude house each night, smiling as if all was well. Raymond vowed in his heart no man would cheat him from the 100 acres he had been promised. If he had to become a thief and ride far away to steal sheep and goats, he would pay his bills. And if Ortiz was a dishonest man and tried to take from Raymond what was his, then Raymond would kill the man. If he would die in the process, then that is the way it must be.

As Raymond rode towards the Ortiz hacienda, his eyes scanned the land around him. It is strange how man settled in one place, he thought looking out over the short stubby pinon trees. Winter was coming and he knew that soon the land would be white with snow. Raymond had not had the time to explore much of the land around him. His friends often told stories of a box canyon filled with horse bones, but he never ventured there. And he had never gone out to the small table-topped peak that they said was covered with ancient drawings. These things did not really interest Raymond. He needed to go out onto the land and find wood for the fire. Grass for his sheep, hidden water holes. Raymond did not have time to think of the past or future. His deepest thoughts were the 100 acres that stretched around his house. He had walked the hundred acres, not exact, he knew, but close. This 100 acre piece of land would be his heart and soul. He could see in years more rooms added to his home. More burros and even a horse. There would be a milk cow and a smoke house. He would dig a deep cellar for the garden. Many of the adobes from the old church were still good and could be reused on his home. The rest of the land around Raymond was a necessity to maintain his 100 acres. Dismounting in the courtyard of the hacienda, Raymond tethered his burro and walked towards the door. "Here I am — your slave," he murmured to himself, hardening his insides to prepare for his tasks.

Sandra reached down and picked up the two water buckets and walked towards the house. She liked to be outdoors on the days her husband was gone. When he was around he was always underfoot. Always needing help. It was good to be alone at times. But when

Raymond was gone, Sandra never felt alone. She would take a few moments each day and do nothing but stand and look at the land around her. Standing alone and quiet it was as though she was surrounded by thousands of ghosts. Ghosts that reached for her but did not make her afraid. Instead they made her feel alive and warm, content. She loved this dried up land. She loved the mountains to the east and the west and the rolling clay hills behind them. She loved the peak in the distance and the old church not more than 200 yards away. As she grew up in Mexico, her father working for a very rich man, she would always remember her father when he was drunk, rambling on and on about the land. Her father would never get his land. Dying in the street one night alone, choking on his own vomit.

Sandra could see for the first time in her life stability, being able to make plans, and see into the future. She knew where she would plant her garden. She knew where she would plant the cottonwood trees. She could see herself as an old woman watching her grandchildren playing. There would be more sheep and more goats and chickens. Around her was her life and the ghosts. The land needed Sandra as much as Sandra needed the land.

Sandra kicked on the front door and stepped into the house with the two water buckets. In a few months she would not be able to do this. She did not yet feel the baby inside of her, but she knew he grew each day. "You will have a home, my little one," she spoke, setting down the water buckets with a slight grunt, "you will have a home and a future."

Raymond stepped up onto the burro. Today he cleaned chimneys. Next week he would split wood for the Ortiz fireplaces. Winter would soon be here. Raymond hoped it would be mild. He did not want any of his sheep to die from the cold. It would be a disaster with no money to replace them.

As he rode the sun set and the coyotes began to howl. Raymond rode thinking about winter and did not feel the ghosts like his wife.

CHAPTER 4
THE JOURNEY

One week after the meeting of all the large land owners, Henrico Ortiz and Fidel Estrada left for the Oklahoma territory. They rode with four armed men as guards and two peons from the hacienda to cook and take care of the animals. Arriving in Lawton, Oklahoma, one month later, they rented a room at a boarding-house, and the next morning went to the office of the company commander. Young Ortiz and Estrada were both used to being listened to and when they were told by the private in the front office that the Colonel would not see them for several days, they became outraged. With this the private stood up and looking at the two Spaniards spoke curtly, "Listen you two Mexican mother-fuckers, here nobody gives a shit where you come from. Now if you want to wait, wait, and if you don't, get the fuck out of here." And for the first time, the two heirs to great fortunes were made to feel as other men.

Later that day walking around the small military town, they were not used to being treated as secondary people. Even the shopkeepers treated them as Mexicans. Henrico, walking back to the boarding house, commented, "These people have no respect for men of bearing." What he did not realize was that the soldiers and white people had no respect for anybody.

The next day, disenchanted they took their proclamation to the company commander's office and gave it to the private. When they had left the office, the private opened the document, read it slowly, and threw it in the garbage. Who did these people think they were?

With winter approaching, the ride back to Santa Fe was cold and slow. Upon returning, Henrico told his father of the treatment they had received, and his father felt his stomach tighten. Standing on his porch that afternoon he looked out upon the great expanse of his domain and knew in his heart there would be no stopping the future. He did not think that this is how the Indians must have felt. He only thought of himself and his father and his father's father.

Over the past month Raymond had worked hard bringing in great quantities of wood for the house and cutting and hauling by hand large amounts of grama grass to feed his sheep and goats during the winter. He had over fifty sheep grazing around the house and many chickens. His wife was beginning to show her pregnancy and with it at times was out of sorts and grouchy, but this did not bother Raymond.

He traded three sheep to a surveyor in Santa Fe who had come out and surveyed his land. Now in each corner he had piled rocks to form markers for his 100 acres. He built a rock wall around a small area that in the spring he would make his garden, and reinforced his buildings for the animals during the winter. He also began construction on a small wagon; in the spring he hoped to buy a horse with money from his sheep crop. From the mountains towards the gold mine he shot several deer with a borrowed rifle. All in all, life was good.

But with Christmas approaching, he did not have the money to go into town and buy something for his wife. He wanted desperately to buy her a new dress or new shoes. A shawl for church or a tiny ring. But there was not enough money for even the cheapest of gifts, and this lay heavy on his heart.

One afternoon Raymond was walking around the old church poking at the crumbling walls and inspecting the ancient adobe bricks for possible reuse. A room for the baby. He walked around the church until he came to what had been the front door. Standing looking at the adobes that used to butt up to the door jamb, a sudden wave of emotion ran through his body like he never felt before. He was so taken aback, he sat down and leaned back against the church. Raymond felt as though the wind had been knocked from him. His heart beat furiously in his chest and his mind reeled in feeings he could not name or define. He dug his fingers into the earth and when he did this, his fingers ran against an old piece of red flagstone. Feeling this, Raymond brushed away the dirt and sand covering the stone. Concentrating on his task, the feelings vanished from within him as fast as they had appeared.

Raymond was delighted. As he moved more and more dirt, he uncovered many flagstones. This would save much work. He could bring the burro here and move the stones and make a walkway for the house. As Raymond uncovered more and more stones, he uncovered one that wiggled when he touched it, and without knowing why, he picked the stone up. When he looked underneath the stone, he dropped the rock in shock. Lying in the dirt was a black spear point like he had never seen before. There were countless pottery fragments and arrowheads on the property.

To Raymond they were nothing. But this, this point was different. Raymond reached out with both hands and making his hands into a cup, scooped the point out of the ground. Here for the first time Raymond felt magic and time. For the first time, Raymond sensed beauty in life. He stood and holding the black obsidian point up to the sun it seemed as though it lived. Inside the glistening point was life and the point seemed to become hot in Raymond's hands and suddenly the love he felt for his wife swept through his body, and it was like a great dam bursting sending the water rushing down the valley without control.

Raymond, clutching the point, began to run up the small rise to the house. He would show this to his wife. But close to the house, Raymond stopped. No, he would not show it to her. He would hide the point, and in his spare time he would build a small box and line the inside with rabbit fur, and he would give this to his wife for Christmas.

Walking to the house he completely forgot about the flagstone walkway. That night eating beans and mutton he was silent and could only think of how he would build the box for the point and what he would carve on it. There would be a star and a moon. There would be a sun on the side. He would carve a mountain on the other side and in the front he would carve a house with a chimney. That night lying in bed by his sleeping wife, Raymond knew a great change had come over him. For the first time in his existence, Raymond knew lying in the darkness that he would die. That all his hopes and his dreams, his labor in the end would be nothing. He would die. There was nothing but land. Land was security. He lay his arm across Sandra and moved his hand slowly to her stomach. Here sleeping and growing was the reason for life. He shut his eyes and the black obsidian swam in his mind's eye. "Ortiz," he murmured before sleep overcame him, "I am not a Mexican dog, I am not a Mexican dog."

CHAPTER 5
THE GOVERNOR

Governor Valdez sat in his office and rubbed his weary brow. Over the past twelve years so many things had changed in his life.

He sat and looked out of his office into the plaza of Santa Fe. Indians milled around covered with turquoise jewelry, wagons sloshed through the early November mud, and traders from all parts of the country wheeled in and out of the various bars and eating establishments. The governor did not like it. It had been so much easier years earlier. More parties, more time to be with his wife and children. Now it was meeting after meeting with the military, meeting after meeting with the landowners. And the fear about the United States. He would just as soon pack his belongings and take his family and move to Mexico. Today Ortiz was coming once again begging for protection. He must think he was an idiot. He knew Henrico Ortiz and Estrada had ridden to Oklahoma. They were like everybody else, they were like him. Ready to grab for any straw to save what was theirs. He hated them, hated Santa Fe, hated Indians and hated being governor. He was growing old and it was time to be able to sit and rest and think about his life. He had enough gold and silver for ten men. Enough to go to Mexico and live under good Spanish law and not work the rest of his life. To hell with the land the king of Spain had given to these people. Let them raise and pay for an army and let them fight for their own land. He knew what he would do if the Americans came. He would gather his small garrison and ride out of here. This place was no place to die for.

Don Ortiz strode briskly into the governor's office. Presumptuous bastard, the governor thought. He did not even knock. Don Ortiz paced nervously around the room. "Well, have you heard from Mexico?" he demanded.

The governor looked at Ortiz. "They have sent world that they cannot help us at the moment. They tell us to do what we must and live in the glory of God and the sovereignty of Spain."

Don Ortiz plopped down in a straight-backed wooden chair. "I was afraid of this."

The governor looked at Don Ortiz and for a moment he could not help but feel sad for him. The power was slowly draining from his body. The governor stood. And with his back to Don Ortiz, he looked out the window. "Maybe when the time comes we should take all our possessions and go to Mexico."

Don Ortiz laughed, "I have never been to Mexico. I was born here, lived here, this is my land. Not Mexico, not a country across the ocean I have never seen. What do I care about Spain or kings or queens or trade routes around the world?"

The governor looked at the man. "With the land you have, Don Ortiz, you are a power and a country yourself. You rule as strong as a country, killing squatters, hanging people who steal from your land, taking tribute from all people who you have promised 100 acres of land. You hire guns to do your work. So don't cry to me about kings and queens. Maybe you should solve your own problems your own way. Don't you understand the king of Spain does not even know where we are? He has troubles at home now." The governor turned and gazed back out the window. "So it is with power, my friend. Power comes and power goes, things taken by the sword leave by the sword. Here we are, a tiny dry piece of land between the United States and the ocean, and we will go to the new power." The governor turned and looked at Ortiz. "It is only a matter of time."

Don Ortiz sat in the La Fonda bar and drank whiskey. The people around him kept a respectable distance and the bartender did not speak. People did not approach or speak to a man of power. That night, riding back to the hacienda, Don Ortiz fell off his horse and broke his neck.

A month later Henrico packed all of the belongings of the Ortiz hacienda on many wagons and taking his mother and two sisters and all the servants, headed for Mexico. He had sold all the sheep and goats and told everybody he would be back within a few years. But people knew he would never return.

Isabella, riding in the wagon, watched the hacienda disappear slowly from her view. She did not cry but sat calmly and remembered Don Ortiz when he was a young man, so dashing and brave on his fine black horse. Turning away from her sight of the home she looked south. It would be good to go to a new place. Good to see new faces and talk to new people. Good not to live with the memories.

Hearing that the Ortizes had left for Mexico, Raymond was filled with a joy like he had never felt. He ran around his land looking at the small bushes and trees. They were his, his for time. His now, not nine years from now. Sandra upon hearing the news began to cry and, holding her swelling stomach, she looked at her husband and spoke, "Raymond, Raymond, my love, my prayers have been answered."

That night the looting of the hacienda began. Everything that could be utilized or had been left behind was taken. Gates and fence posts, piled up wood, rocks from fireplaces and adobes.

Within a week the hacienda looked like vultures had picked its bones. Over the next years the wind would blow through its broken windows and the rats and mice would take over the once stately home.

CHAPTER 6
THE CHRISTMAS GIFT

Raymond built a work shed out of the rough shelter he and his wife had lived in before construction of the house. Here he kept his tools and the many useful items he had taken from the Ortiz hacienda. Taking from the hacienda he had not felt like a thief but more like a man taking what was his. Raymond sat close to the small fireplace in the corner and in his hands he held the black flashing spear point. He did not know what it was exactly, but the spear point held a power over him. He could sit and look into the deep darkness of the point and it was as though there was no world, no time, no worries about his sheep or goats, the new baby. Raymond lay the point down and picked up the small cedar box he had built. On the left side of the box he had carved a sun and on the right side he carved a moon. On the back he carved a small flowing river by a mountain, and on the front a small sheep. Now on the top he was carving a house with a chimney.

Slowly and with great deliberation he moved the small knife, forming the lines of the house. There was never a fear in his heart Sandra would not like the spear point. Surely she too would feel the magic and the love that emitted from the point. Raymond worked and was lost to the howl of the cold wind that swirled around the small house and kicked the freezing snow up into the air. Raymond was happy, there was enough wood and food for the family and animals to last the winter. For the first time in his life, Raymond was his own man, caretaker of his own destiny. The 100 acres around him was his. There was no landlord, no man demanding his labor and payment to live. Each day he would stand in front of his small home and look out upon his land and it was as though the land was his god. There was no heaven and hell, there was only this small piece of earth. And with the earth a future. A future to dream and plan. A place to build and grow old and one day be buried. There was no need for a God when one owned property. Raymond moved the knife slowly, taking small pieces of the cedar wood to form the walls and chimney of the house. Beside him the point lay motionless and timeless.

Sandra sat by the wooden table and looked into the fire. The house was warm and cozy, which she was thankful for. This land was cold in the winter, so unlike her home in Mexico. But even cold it was her land. Deep inside she did not think of the land as hers and her husband's. It was hers, an integral part of her being and the life she held within herself. It was different to be poor and possess something, far different from being rich and acquiring another possession.

To her the land was a stepping stone to heaven. A gift from God she had seen and felt when they had first looked out over the abandoned church months earlier. She had told Raymond he should not tear down the old church and even the flagstone he had hauled up for a walkway from the church she did not like. Unlike her husband, Sandra held a deep conviction of time in her heart. There were spirits in old things, life forces still moving and feeling. At all times she felt the ghosts around her. At times she would reach down and pick up pieces of broken pottery and she could see the women working and talking, hear the children playing beside them, and she felt as though she could reach out and touch these people and say to them, See, I too live, we are as one.

Several weeks earlier she had ridden out on the burro one day while Raymond was out looking for the sheep. She had ridden out to the tabletop peak not far from the house. For some reason she was always drawn to the peak but had always been too busy to go. But this afternoon she stopped everything she was doing and went. Standing by the peak, she was overwhelmed by the pictographs she saw. She had no idea how old they were or by whom they had been painstakingly drawn, but she could feel emitting from the rock the power of the drawings. But what amazed her the most was the horse and above the horse the simple cross, as if the cross blessed the horse. The horse was more alive than the other scrapings. This horse had been drawn by a man who knew horses. There was a horse that to this day lived and breathed and touched the earth with flying hooves. Standing looking at the horse, Sandra realized that people as simple as she had drawn these animals and looking around her she could see the Indians upon the land and she could see the Spaniards riding across this land, and she could also see herself and her husband upon the land. And she realized she was but a progression upon the face of the earth. But she also realized she was not an end but a small step leading to some unknown destiny. There was a power that pulled mankind along. A power that set people at different times in the same places and bewildered them with time and confusion.

That night after visiting the peak she dreamt a strange dream. A dream of fire and burning and chaos with strange figures hidden by shadows without faces and forms that filled her with fear and dread. She did not tell her husband of the dream. But tried to rationalize it as being a result of her pregnancy.

Sitting gazing into the fire, Sandra could feel the baby kick inside her stomach. It was a good feeling, a deep feeling of life that she could not put into words. She stood and walked into the other room. In this part of the house it was cooler. She undressed slowly and put on her nightgown. Lying down on the bed she inhaled deeply and exhaled slowly.

Raymond lay the box down and admired it in the flickering glow from the kerosene lantern. It was not a great work of art. His figures were crude and childlike, but the box emitted a warmth that told of the labor and concentration. Standing and looking at the point and the box, Raymond was happy. It would be good to go to his wife now and make love to her, but there had been no love making in over a month and would be none for a while longer. Raymond shrugged and laughed to himself. There should be a way man could make love and not worry about making women pregnant. Blowing out the lantern, Raymond walked through the cold night to the house. My house, he thought, opening the door, you are very good to me.

Raymond stood and looked down on the sleeping form of his wife. She seemed to be contented and at peace. He looked at her often in her sleep. Wondering where she went with her dreams. Watching as her lips would twitch and her eyelids flutter. It was at these times he would feel his greatest love for her. Times when he could not touch or speak to her. He felt like a child standing over her sleeping form. Sandra was Raymond's complete life. Without her there would be no need for land. Without her there would be no need for anything. Raymond undressed slowly and lay down beside his sleeping, dreaming wife.

Lying down Raymond watched the fire dance across the ceiling. Ever since finding the point he had noticed things in his life he had never noticed before. Fire dancing across the ceiling or the touch of the wind on the cedar and juniper trees. There came to his senses a motion and a fluidness to the world around him. These things in his simple mind he could not label or define but they were a feeling, a deep peaceful feeling that made the toil and work of his days lose their bitterness. Raymond rolled over and kissed the swelling breast of his wife and rolled back over and shut his eyes. Within the darkness there were no ghosts or memories, no dreams or desires, only the love of his wife and the warmth she spread through their bed.

During the night clouds rolled in to block the sun and several inches of snow fell upon the land. Rising early, Sandra slipped quietly from the bed as not to disturb Raymond. Going outside she stood and looked out upon the fresh snow. There were no footprints or animal prints to disturb the snow. She stood and looked and the world seemed fresh and alive, untouched and unblemished. Standing she turned her gaze to the old church, and before her stood a small round man with a long brown robe. He was smiling and in his hand he held a black spear point. Sandra went back into the house and started the fire. The vision of the priest burned in her mind. He looked so happy, so full of love, and Sandra took it as a sign to her from God that all would be well in her life. Raymond rose from the bed and could smell the deep aroma of coffee and tortillas. Walking into the other room he noticed the good mood his wife was in. Turning from her cooking Sandra smiled a deep warm smile. "My husband," she murmured, "God is with us."

After eating, Raymond went to his workshop and finished carving the cedar box. Painstakingly he fit the rabbit fur into the box and then he took the point and lay it on the fur. Looking into the box it was as though he was looking at his own beating heart. Sandra, my love, he thought, I give to you my greatest treasure.

December 24, Raymond and Sandra bundled up and with Raymond walking and Sandra riding the burro they went to the Ortiz hacienda. Here in the old chapel which had not been destroyed by the people, a priest would say midnight mass. Before leaving Raymond went back into the house, and taking the box out of his coat, he placed it on the wooden table for Sandra to find when they returned. Traveling over the land with the night, Raymond was filled with great emotion. It seemed as though he had never seen the land as he did now. His feet crunching the fresh snow were as the footsteps of all men. His heart reaching out to his wife also extended to the stars and the moon. And sitting in the small chapel as the priest said mass in Latin, he shut his eyes and a great peace swept over his body. Leading his wife riding the burro home after the mass, he felt as if he were Joseph. When they arrived home, Raymond put the burro in its corral and threw it some grass. Going inside Sandra was sitting by the table and in her lap was the small carved cedar box, and in her hands was the black obsidian spear point. Tears rolled down her cheeks and she was so lost in the point she did not hear or see Raymond. She sat holding the point and wave after wave of emotion ran over her body and in her mind swam the vision of the priest she had seen by the church. The point seemed to pulsate in her hands, and it was like a crucifix telling of love and hope, sadness and despair. Her eyes clouded with tears, she looked up and saw Raymond and between sobs she spoke, "It is so beautiful my love, it is timeless like we are." Raymond went to her side and falling to his knees he buried his head in her side. "It is all I can give you my little one." Sandra rubbed her hand through his coarse dark hair and smiled. "You have given me far more than any gift, you have given me of yourself."

Outside the stars slowly faded with the approaching day and once again, the earth awoke with a new dream and a new promise.

CHAPTER 7
THE AMERICAN SOLDIERS

General John Gunther sat in the stagecoach and watched the rolling Oklahoma land pass by. It was good to be getting back West. Another week in Washington and he would have gone crazy. He hated the balls and receptions, bowing to the women and acting like such a fine gentleman. That was what was wrong with the army today. There were far too many fancy Dans with polished boots and brass standing at parties trying to impress the women instead of out fighting wars like they were supposed to. For the past three days on the stagecoach he did not shave nor button the top button of his uniform. If shaving and a buttoned uniform were the true story of a soldier, then the army could forget it! But the General did have one fond memory of Washington. A certain diplomat's young daughter. Well-bred and raised, she was like the rest of the

Washington set. Talking about teas and socials and who knew who and what. But she had liked the General. Walking over to him and introducing herself. He danced with her several times and was amazed at the softness of her side and the perfume that floated around his head. It was a quick easy seduction, very delightful. She would marry some young West Point graduate one day and never remember him, but he knew there would be nights out in the wilderness he would think about her young pert breasts and soft stomach.

The General had never been married, never really fallen in love. There was only the army in his life. The true fighting army. He had volunteered and been given outpost camps all over the West. From Kansas to North Dakota to Oklahoma territory. Wherever the action was he went. There was nothing in life like the battle, no feeling or emotions that came over man like war. War was the true test of man, man's destiny, the General knew. Man was not a peaceful creature. He was no better than an animal except he could reason. Man was a cunning creature that if he was weak, would be ruled by another man. Only the strong controlled their destiny. Only the strong could hold onto freedom. Give me 150 of the coldest meanest men in the world, and I could conquer the west. Drive all the way to California, the General thought.

The General puffed on his cigar. He felt good. With his new orders and out away from the real world, life was good. He could not wait to reach the post and tell his men about their new assignment. The men had been growing restless lately. Over the past two years they had more than subdued the Indians in the area. Now homesteaders streamed into the territory. Building homes and barns, putting up corrals and fences. There were new schools and even more women. But now the soldiers were reduced to a mere police capacity. Running off to chase down a few brave bucks from the reservation. There were no more large operations. No attacks on the Indians. It was time for a lesser commander to come in with fresh young green troops who could write letters home to their girl friends about being in the West and how dangerous it was. But now there was a new territory, an area of land, and he was going to lead the force that would take it from the Spanish. The General in his mind's eye saw his men mounting their horses, swords clanking as they mounted. He heard the crack of the leather harness as the mules pulled to start the canon moving and the wagons filled with supplies and powder. He could see the flags rippling with the wind and feel the surge of power and control he felt when his army moved before him. His will, his convictions. His decisions brought life and death and this in all of his being was the essence of his life. His power over life and death.

The Indians of the Oklahoma territory hated him. He was a mean cruel man. He was not a man of his word. He hung as many Indians as he could and shot many more. He showed no remorse about killing men, women or children — they were all enemy. The young were but enemies yet to grow. The women the ones to create new enemies. Indians caught off the reservation were shot. Shot without trial or explanation, just shot and left to lie for the buzzards and coyotes. The General was not a believer in the means of action but in the results. Winning is what counted, completion of the mission. Making this easy and possible was deep within the General a deep hatred for all of man except the white race. Indians were not people, Mexicans were not people, and Spaniards should be back in Spain.

As the stagecoach continued and the sun set, the General sipped from a whiskey bottle. He knew he drank too much, but the pleasure of drink was not too much to ask. It was cheap and easy and brought sleep.

Two days later the General got off the stage in Lawton, Oklahoma. Around him the post bustled with activity. He was met by Colonel Andres and Captain Silar, both good hard soldiers like himself. Both loners who also liked battle. The General smiled deeply, returning the two men's salutes.

"Gentlemen," he spoke, "we will be leaving this godforsaken country, we have a rendezvous with the Spanish."

Riding through the post on his black horse, the General breathed deep the smell of horses and men. Listened for sounds of stomping boots and sergeants giving orders. Discipline, there must always be discipline, he preached to his officers. If a man thinks he can get away with something, let him try, but if he is caught, the punishment must be swift and severe. With this creed, the General soon weeded out the weak from his ranks and replaced them with strong, tough men like himself, men wishing to fight. Of his men the General never asked questions. If a man was wanted back in the real world for murder, well, that was his problem. The General asked for fighters, men without fear and in return in time his men followed him, knowing he was like them. In all battles the General was always in the battle. He did not lay back with field glasses and

116

watch. "Blood and Guts," his men called him behind his back. Did you see old Blood and Guts cut that Indian's head off with his sword? But although the General was a tough man, he did not allow mutilation of the enemy bodies. All dead were left alone. And for this the Indian enemies respected him. He was a true man who walked across the face of the earth without the blessing of God. He was indeed a power to be reckoned with.

The General sat in his office and watched out the window as the flag was brought down for the evening. The flag, he smirked. Allegiance to the flag was such a childish notion. There were no flags, only personal wants and desires. We are men pulled by destiny, not by flags. A true fighter had no belief in flags, only in fighting, only the feeling that came over one after the battle. Only the slowly diminishing odds of staying alive for another rendezvous with death.

The General walked outside and walked through the garrison. On the outskirts of the post were the many bars and whorehouses. There was a certain little Mexican whore he wished to see. Her hands could bring the tightness out of his neck and quell the fire that burnt within him. He laughed as he walked — women, they're all whores in their own way. They all sell out for something.

The General lay beside the sleeping form of Rosalina. Spring seemed like an eternity away. There would be a new commander with his troops arriving in the spring. And with their arrival he and his men would ride out towards Santa Fe. He wished he could muster his men and leave right this moment. Have the bugle sound and take off with just swords and rifles. He wished his horses could fly up and over the land and set them down in the middle of the enemy's camp, and most of all he wished the enemy would not want to surrender. In his nostrils he could smell the odor of gunpowder and the cries of wounded men. He could see the blood of man run out onto the ground and hear the moan of the wind, sweeping over the battlefield. The General rolled over on his side and shook the sleeping girl. He cupped her breast in his hand and kissed the dark nipple. Spring, he thought, come to me quickly.

Raymond worked with another man from a nearby homestead. He was such as himself. A poor Mexican who had also come up out of Mexico. It was April, and winter was leaving the land and the men worked with a new freshness to their bodies. During the winter Raymond built a small cart and the two men went back and forth, filling the cart with flat stones and then back to the mouth of the box canyon. The canyon would be perfect for trapping the sheep. Already the canyon's mouth was three-quarters shut off by the four-foot high rock wall. Here after trapping the sheep the men could cull out the ones for sale and release the others back onto the land. Manuel placed a rock in place and stood up, stretching his back. "I work and work, I sleep with my wife and it is work, we have more babies and it is more work, it is all work." Raymond laughed. "Well, let's go rob the gold mine and then we will no longer work."

Manuel grinned a large toothless grin. "I said I work, I did not say I was stupid."

"And how is your new baby?" Manuel asked, stacking another stone.

Raymond grunted, moving a large rock. "She is like the spring," he mused. "Round and plump and healthy like her mother. Her cries are like bird songs."

Manuel rubbed his whisker-covered face. "That is good, my friend," he spoke, "but wait until there are six of them and the bird songs you hear now are the sounds of crows." And he laughed a deep happy laugh.

Raymond changed the subject. "Have you been to Santa Fe recently?" Manuel shook his head, no. Raymond continued, "It has grown immensely. There are people from all over there now, Americans trading, Comanches from the south bringing goods out of Mexico. It seems as though it is out of control. The Spaniards have lost the power and stand around like sheep. There is a rumor the Americans will soon come and take over this land."

"It does not concern us, my friend," Manuel answered. "The Americans will not bother people as you and me. There is nothing we have that they want. That is one good thing about being poor. Nobody cares about you, you have nothing to steal, so they leave you alone. The poor will always be the poor."

Raymond turned the burro and started back for another load of rocks. It was strange, but he no longer felt poor. True, he did not have any money. But he had sheep and goats and a cart now. He had a home and corrals and a wife and child. He had more food than he had ever had in his life. No, he told himself, I am not poor. Poor is something the rich man would call me, but I am not poor.

Raymond walked and was oblivious to the pottery fragments and arrowheads lying on the ground. Looking out upon the land he could see the new growth beginning to green, but it was much sparser than last year. Which was strange, because there had been more than enough moisture during the winter for the grass to grow.

"Manuel," Raymond spoke, "does the grass look thin this year?"

Manuel looked out upon the land. "The grass always grows, Raymond. The grass is a gift from God."

But looking at the grass, Raymond could not help but feel a pang of anxiety creep through his stomach.

CHAPTER 8
THE INVASION

General Gunther would not leave Oklahoma for one year — one long and bitter year. Each week he waited anxiously for the letter, telling him the replacement troops were on the way but each week there was no word. When he did receive a letter it was just another delay. The post was an endless procession of inspections and small field drills to keep the troops in shape. With each passing month the General seemed to slip deeper and deeper into despair. He began to drink heavily and spend more time with the prostitutes. He had gone over the various routes to Santa Fe on the maps so many times he could shut his eyes and see them.

In the winter, the replacements finally arrived and with a small ceremony the General handed over power of the post. For the next three weeks the General moved his troops out onto the plains and bivouacked. Here they drilled and he mustered his troops once again into fighting condition. Walking through tents and watching the drills and rifle practice, the General once again felt the blood run through his veins and the old feelings of power and glory enter his mind.

Sitting one afternoon in his tent with his junior officers sipping brandy, the General was in a good mood. "I have heard," he said, "Santa Fe is heavily protected by some of the Spanish's finest soldiers."

A junior officer spoke enthusiastically, "It should be no problem for us. We have superior rifles, superior cannons and superior men." Outside the steady roar of cannon practice split the air.

"Sergeant Thrush can shoot a tick off of a hound dog with his cannon," another officer laughed.

The general held up his brandy glass, "To the company," he spoke, "to the battle." The officers stood and clanked their glasses together.

Two weeks later as the replacement band played a military march, the General and his men moved slowly off into the horizon. There were 145 men, eight cannons, and ten wagons of powder and shot, with four wagons of supplies. Most of the food would be taken as they progressed. Cattle, sheep and goats along the way would be sacrificed in the name of conquest and the United States. Like all armies they marched under the impression of righteousness and glory and deliverers of truth.

Riding, the General felt complete once again. He was a soldier venturing out into the unknown, testing fate and luck with a smile. After a month and a half, the General made camp a mere mile from Santa Fe. He took a day and positioned his cannon and looked at the land, deciding on the best way to attack. The next day he sent an envoy into town to approach the Governor and the Post Commander. The envoy returned several hours later and looking at the General grimly spoke. "The soldiers and the governor have left, sir, the city is ours."

The General bit into his cigar and exhaled deeply, "Chicken-shit mother-fuckers," he spat, "chicken-shit mother-fuckers."

The next afternoon he rode into Santa Fe with his army and made headquarters in the Spanish garrison and put his office in the Governor's palace that had been left completely stocked with food. For the General there would never be another battle, never the smell of gunsmoke or the cries of men. He would sit enforcing the law for several more years, and then in his old age be sent back to Washington. There he would become like all the other old generals. Attending the teas and socials, telling tales of grand battles and victories and seducing the rich daughters and wives of Washington. He would die ten years later in his sleep in a small boardinghouse room filled with mementos and ribbons. There would be no children to cry over his grave or wife to say he was a good man. There would be a simple ceremony, attended by three soldiers who had served under him and a cold winter wind.

During his time in Santa Fe new treaties would be signed with the Indians giving them specific land surrounding the pueblos they inhabited. The Spanish land grants would be dissolved and surveyors would travel dividing the land into sections. In time this land would be opened up for homesteading, but for now it lay unused. The Mexican squatters were left alone. They would move their sheep back and forth across the land and try to stay as far away as possible from the soldiers that patrolled the area. The Ortiz gold mine was taken over by the United States and the gold sent back to the mint in Kansas. In Mexico the Ortiz family would become rich farmers, continuing as they always had. A family of power with many servants and a fine home.

By 1848 Raymond and Sandra had three children, two girls and one boy. But around them the land was dry and barren of good grass. With the years of sheep and no grass management, the land no longer yielded up sustenance for the animals and then with three years of drought, things were very bad. Raymond had started to drink heavily and at times even beat his children in desperation.

It was a late fall afternoon when a small band of Indians from a pueblo north of Santa Fe raided the homestead. They shot Raymond by the sheep corral and dragged Sandra out in front of the house and raped her repeatedly until she died. The children they lassoed and dragged behind their horses until they were but bloody balls of flesh and bone. With this they threw kerosene in all the buildings and set them ablaze.

A small carved box sitting in the windowsill would catch fire, and when the roof partially caved in, a black obsidian spear point would fall into the ashes and remains of the rock house. The rock walls of the structures would remain to withstand the cold winters and winds of summer.

Soldiers hearing about the massacre would ride out and seeing the ruins and finding the bodies, they would bury the dead and poke around the ruins for a few moments and ride off. One rider would mutter, ''Just some poor Mexicans,'' and think about the Indian whore he was going to see in the evening.

Within a few years the remaining Mexican homesteaders would no longer hold onto their land. They could not sell it as it did not belong to them and their overgrazing had left the land devoid. Life for them became as it had back in Mexico. They were but peons in another man's land. Landless and homeless they worked for the army or lived miserable lives living off the deer and elk high in the mountains.

The Americans opened up trade routes and Santa Fe became a center for trade in the West. Kit Carson came and made Santa Fe his headquarters. Indians from the south traded and Mexicans from Mexico traded. New homes arose and new stores. The army sent in more troops who protected the trade routes and subdued a few mild Indian uprisings.

Across the ruined church and pueblo and the Ortiz hacienda, the wind blew and the snows fell. Devil's Peak stood motionless and silent, and the horse still seemed alive and blessed. Raymond's rock home withstood time, and the spear point lay motionless and timeless, uncaring and unseeing to the world around it . . . waiting for another time and another place.

BOOK FOUR
THE COWBOYS

After the invasion of the Spanish-held territories, the land opened up for the new race in power. Thieves and murderers, people with no hope and seeking to forget their history, came West. They came and settled, and as in the dream of Man of Darkness, they fenced in the land. Unlike the Spanish who claimed all the land, the new people claimed parcels as theirs. These parcels were called ranches, and within the boundary of the ranch, the owner was as strong and powerful as any king or president. The Mexican was pushed into servitude for the new rulers, and the Indian was forced onto specific tracts of inhospitable land known as reservations. Here he stayed hanging tenaciously to a life that progress and time passed by. These new people would become labeled as cowboys. They were a strong, independent people who looked to no man for help and to the land for their life.

CHAPTER 1
THE HISTORY — 1948 A.D.

Grandfather Simpson sat on the porch of the brick home. It was a nice home. A home with gas heat and a refrigerator, a bathroom and running water. He smiled remembering the house he had been born in. It had been four adobe rooms, no running water, the walk to the outhouse cold and freezing in the winter. He remembered chopping wood for days, always trying to find a way to slip away but always under the watchful eye of his father or mother. It had been hard, he supposed, but it had also been good. There were no gas guzzling tractors, or pickup trucks. He had worked the fields for weeks with an old plow horse and a one-way plow. Worked for weeks to do what a tractor could now do in a day.

The old house was gone now, torn down, and this new beautiful modern home built in its place. Across the way from the porch were three stallion runs and down to the east, a large barn with concrete floor. Behind the house was the bunkhouse and cook's kitchen for the cowboys. And everywhere were the tall majestic cottonwood trees his mother had planted when he was still a baby. They grew over 50 feet tall, shading the bunkhouse, keeping the hot searing sun away during the summer. Each day was a chorus of songs from the birds and the endless music from the wind rustling through the leaves.

Grandfather Simpson sat and remembered. "God, old man," he muttered to himself. "Seventy-nine years old, seventy-nine and all this has happened."

To the east of the house he could hear the steady roar of the tractor as his son prepared the April soil for an oat crop. Inside the house Bill's wife worked in the kitchen. Mary was a good woman. A hard-working lady. So different from most women these days. Grandfather rubbed his brow, remembering his wife. Poor Lisa, he thought, worked your life to death, never saw anything but this land. Saw babies born and children die. Always wanted to see parts of the world — Greece, Italy, but only saw this land. It had been much harder then. Living on the land one was chained to the land. Going into town with a wagon once a month or once every two months, loading up with supplies and seeing people, was a major event. It was only twenty-six miles to Santa Fe. Twenty-six miles of oiled road now from the front gate which was five miles from the house. But then it had taken two days by wagon if the weather was right. One rain and a man could mire a wagon for days. Now a man could jump in a truck and be in town in thirty minutes, get his business done and be back home before the sun was down.

It still amazed Grandpa. Time moved so quickly and man advanced even faster. He felt good sitting on the porch. The war was finally over. His son was back home in one piece. A little quieter, carrying in his heart some deep grief he never talked about. But he was home. He really didn't know how he and Mary and the two boys had kept the ranch going during the war. Mary had worked harder than three men. Feeding cattle, taking care of sick calves, riding like any cowboy in the spring and fall. Always smiling and talking. But there were nights when he could hear her cry in her room. Soft sobs, so very alone and distant. Grandpa could see the fear in her eyes when mail came to the post office in Lamy. But the dreaded letter of death never came and one morning Bill had been at the door. Everybody cried, Mary, the boys and Grandpa. With time it all seemed like a bad dream that occurred years ago. The ranch was whole again, there were no dark shadows and Grandpa could spend his last days like an old man should — sitting on the porch and thinking about his life and talking to the children.

Brad and Joe ran around the corner of the house and scampered to the porch. Brad plopped down on the swing and spoke excitedly, "Come on, Grandpa, you told us in a few minutes, tell us about the ranch." Grandpa rubbed the head of six year old Joe and faked a punch at Brad sitting on the step — Brad was eight. "Okay, okay, you two have me cornered," Grandpa looked at the cottonwood trees and a deep far away look came into his eyes before speaking.

"My father took all of his money and his young wife and bought a wagon and several oxen. He left Kansas City in the spring of 1858, headed for he did not know where. Things were bad in Kansas City, there was no hope and he figured dying out in the wilderness was better than dying a slow death caught up in some city. How he ended up here I really don't know, he never talked about it much. I only know that they withstood Indian attacks, sickness and much hunger getting here and this is the place they got to and wished to travel no farther. My father built a small adobe house here on the spot this home is on now. They lived here for the first winter and had to eat their oxen to survive. In the spring of the first year he rode out on a horse and in the corners of this ranch he piled rocks into tall spirals and swore that this was

125

his land and no man would ever take it from him.

"From the mountaintop over there by the gold mine to the edge of the old Ortiz hacienda south for miles past Devil's Peak, he claimed as his. During the summer he filed with the government and within a year he had this land deeded in his name. My father fought off renegade Indians from the reservation, Mexican bandits, bad weather, disease, drought and everything imaginable to keep this land. He worked his whole life from dawn until dusk. His hands were hard as granite and his back bowed from labor. He was a tough man, a man who could kill another man but he was a fair man. I remember when he started hiring cowboys and they first started to build fence over this ranch." With this Grandfather chuckled, "It's not easy building fence on 38,000 acres of land. The cowboys treated him with respect. He was a fair honest man who payed his men when he said he would but expected a hard day from each man. When I was born my older brother had already died from fever and that is about all I know about him. They never spoke about him much, but I know they loved him deeply. From the time I was eight years old, I worked every day with my father."

Brad jumped up from the swing and began to run off, "Tell us more later, Grandpa," and with that he and Joe were off to another adventure. Grandfather laughed, hell, they'd heard the story one thousand times if they had heard it once. It was a good life to be young on a ranch. Able to run through the fields and go out and explore the land. It was far different from living in some fucked up town with all the fucked up people behaving like ants. Grandfather stood and walked into the house and went into the kitchen. He had never told the boys the true reason his father left Kansas City. He had killed a man and escaped from jail. It was strange, but back then a man had a place to go for a new life.

Grandfather walked into the kitchen and Mary was finishing off a load of dishes. Beside her holding fast to her leg was Frank. Grandfather felt a pang of sadness enter his heart. Poor little Frank, he was so small. His features were like those of a tiny doll. He was four years old now and still did not try to say words or speak. He did not laugh or seem to know anything was alive in the world. His two older brothers both young strong strapping boys payed him little attention. And Bill, no matter his effort, could not seem to make himself pick up or hold his youngest child. The child was like another part of Mary. She coddled him, and spoke to him and stroked his head as though he was a small dog. And in turn the boy would look at her with his large sad brown eyes and stick his thumb in his mouth and show no emotion.

Bill had mentioned once the boy should be sent away to a special school, but Mary had gone into a fit and would not listen to a word of it. Grandpa knew Bill did not love the boy. He showered his love on the other two sons but could not force himself to get close to the youngest. Grandpa patted the head of the strange tiny boy and kissed Mary on the cheek. Mary smiled, "Have you seen those two wild ones today?" "Saw them for a while, but then they were off chasing Indians or something." Mary dried her hands on a dish towel and picked up Frank and squeezed him tightly. Frank did not take his thumb out of his mouth or seem to notice the movement.

"Oh, Grandpa," Mary asked, "Do you think he'll ever come into the world?"

Grandpa did not answer. Mary carried the child out into the yard and set him down in a pile of sand. Grandpa sat down on a wooden bench with her and watched the boy. "He loves the sand," Mary said. "He can sit for hours moving it with his hands."

"Maybe he'll be a good farmer," Grandpa mused, "A farmer has to know the land."

Mary looked out beyond the cottonwood trees and scanned the horizon. She loved this ranch but at times it seemed like such a trap. It was always work, and when one thought the work was caught up, it was more work. She looked once more back to the boy playing in the sand and talked more to herself than to Grandfather. "He is so like the land, so quiet and still, it is like time does nothing to him." Mary ran her fingers through her blonde hair. "I feel old. Thirty-eight and I feel old." Grandfather smiled looking at his daughter-in-law. "Don't rush yourself, Mary, you'll be old soon enough."

In the background they could hear the tractor shut down. "Bill's done now," Mary spoke, "Time for me to start dinner. Will you watch the boy?" Grandpa nodded his head. The boy reached out and picked up tiny handfuls of sand and let the sand trickle back into the pile. He did not giggle or make noises, but Grandfather knew the child enjoyed this. Grandfather sat and watched the boy and soon it was as though he was inside the boy, and he felt peaceful and calm. There were no words, no noises. Only the feel of the sand and the touch of the slight spring breeze. You are a strange one, Grandfather thought, but you are a thinker and a

127

feeler and one day you will speak and the deep silence you carry in your heart will melt away.

Grandpa heard Bill close the wooden gate and walk into the yard. The two oldest boys ran to him and grabbed his legs. Bill laughed and tossed them up in the air and held one in a headlock. If only Frank were strong and healthy, Grandpa thought. Bill scooted the two boys away, walked over and stood by the bench and looked at the tiny boy in the sandbox. He then turned his eyes to his father and bowing his head slightly and without speaking, walked into the house to wash up. Across the way several cowboys were riding in after checking fence for the day. Grandpa stood and went over and picked up the boy. He was as light as a feather. It was as though the wind would carry him away if you did not hold him down. Frank looked into the eyes of his grandfather and slowly released the last handful of sand.

Bill gulped his food down in large bites. After dinner he wanted to check the fence the workers were supposed to be doing, and he wanted to check the new angus bull he had bought. Somewhere there were also six cows about to calve that he had not been able to find. He figured they were somewhere over by the old church and the crumbling Mexican homesteader's shack. Brad and Joe kicked at each other under the table to nobody's dismay. Frank sat in his highchair silent and quiet, picking up his food and gingerly putting small portions in his mouth. Mary ate quietly, enjoying the rest. If she wasn't cooking or doing dishes, she was doing laundry. Only during dinner did she really relax. Grandfather watched the family and listened to the small talk about the ranch. Bill was excited, gas would be in full quantity this year and tires for the machinery would be easy to get. He was going to put in 150 acres of alfalfa and try to dig a ditch from the river to fill a pond he had dug during the winter. With this water he could flood his alfalfa field. With enough alfalfa he could keep more cattle during the winter and not have to worry about over-grazing the delicate land.

Grandfather spoke, "When my father came out here there was not a blade of grass left on this land. All the years the Spaniards were here and then the Mexicans, they knew nothing about rotating their sheep. They thought the grass would grow forever, but the sheep cut the grass to the nub and the grass did not grow. My dad was the first rancher in the area to fence the land and cross fence it and move his cattle from area to area always being careful not to let the cattle ruin the land. It took many years before he could build the land back to where he could run a decent herd."

Bill spoke, chewing his food. "A couple of bad years and this place could fold up now, Dad. This old rock dry land with all the clay is fragile as it ever was."

Grandpa looked at Frank eating quietly and laughed. "So it is, I suppose, living on the land is a hard business."

"In a lot of ways it might have been easier when you were young, Dad — no goddamn machinery breaking down, no government regulations, no need of gas, no taxes, no large vet bills."

Mary looked at her husband. "Your boys will say that when you're old, Bill. How it was easier."

Bill smiled at his wife, "You're probably right," he spoke, "right as usual."

"But no matter what," Grandfather added, "there's nothing like the land. It's all a man really has."

Mary looked at Frank not eating now but sitting quietly watching with his deep brown eyes the people around him. She wished so he would cry or smile, frown, anything to show some life. But looking at her silent son, she knew man was more than the land. Man was the stars and the heavens and the oceans. Man was all things he could see and feel. Grandpa and Bill and the two older boys were of the land. It was all they knew, but there were so many things to do with life beside punch cows and plow dirt and raise horses. It was not everything.

Grandpa stood up from the table, and looking at Brad and Joe he motioned for them to follow. "All right, you two hellcats," he spoke, "you wanted to hear one more story before you go to bed."

Sitting in the living room, Grandpa rubbed his face and looked at the boys. "I know — have I ever told you boys about the lost gold on this ranch?" The boys shook their heads in unison, no. Mary walked in and set Frank down on the floor and went back to the kitchen. Grandpa continued.

"Before my father came out here, a man named Ortiz had all the land one can see in every direction. He also owned the gold mine that is still producing on the mountain. Ortiz was a very rich man, and he had many Mexican families living on the land who worked for him. One of the old men who used to live on this ranch told my father this story.

"There is a legend that a bandit in Mexico heard about the Ortiz gold mine, and he rode his horse and mules all the way up here to rob the mine. The story goes he crawled on his belly for over a mile and hid in the trees for a week, watching the men from the mine. He figured out when men changed shifts and when the gold was ready to ship into town to be sent to Mexico. People said he was a handsome young man who was not a bad man but was very poor and could no longer stand to see his family wear rags and his children go hungry.

"One morning he rode down on the men taking the gold to Santa Fe, and killed all but one of them who rode out into the desert. The bandit had three mules with him, and he put all the gold he could on his mules. Story goes many men robbed the Ortiz mine, but none ever got away except this man.

"When I was a boy, there was an old sheriff in town who swears a man robbed the gold mine but was never caught. The Mexican who told the story to my father believed the bandit's gold was left on this ranch. He thought the bandit knew he could not outrun the posse from the mine, and he buried his gold on the ranch to go back to Mexico and return when it was safe. But he never returned, and the gold is still here."

Brad looked at the old man, "Do you think the gold is here, Grandpa?"

Grandpa scratched his head. "When I was a boy, every chance I had I went looking for that gold. I used to dream about finding the gold and being rich, but I really don't know — maybe it is and maybe it isn't. Guess after all the years, no one will ever really find out if the story is true or not."

Joey stood up, "I would have liked to be a bandit."

Grandpa laughed. "You're a bandit now, you rascal," and he reached out and grabbed the boy and began tickling him.

Bill drove the pickup quickly over the dirt road. He wanted to find those cows. Six calves would bring in several thousand dollars and several thousand dollars right now would come in handy. He needed a baler for the alfalfa and some more wire and wages for the cowboys. It was hard keeping up with the ranch. Thirty-eight thousand acres was a large responsibility. At times the only reason he continued was for his boys. They were two strong good hard-working boys who would keep the ranch when he was gone.

He drove by an old Spanish church, the walls still intact after all the years. He had cut a dirt road below the sloping clay cliff that came down from the mesa top by the church and the bulldozer had run through a few of the Indian ruins that sat by the church. Bill had never payed the ruins much attention. He had walked through them a few times, picking up arrowheads and pottery pieces but they did not mean anything to him. They were interesting and the boys liked them, but they were just old things. They had nothing to do with paying the bills or healing sick cows or buying a good breeding bull. They were just something on the land. It was like the Mexican rock house, close to the ruins — they were there, just there. Bill rode around and did not see the cows. He would have to go out with the two hands on horseback and check out the draws and gulleys. Taking another dirt road that crisscrossed the land, Bill checked the fence. The cowboys were doing a good job. He knew they hated making fence. It was demeaning work for a cowboy. They would just as soon be doing the dishes than working on fence.

Bill parked the truck and stepped outside. Across a small draw he could see the new bull. He looked at the land as the sun set. For a few moments everything seemed peaceful and at rest. On the horizon Devil's Peak loomed in the growing darkness. He had not been there in years. He'd ridden by it a million times, but never stopped. When he was a boy he would go there all the time, crawling around on the rock. From the top one could look out for hundreds of miles and see each corner of the ranch.

He got back into the truck and in his mind's eye he could see the horse on the peak. It was funny but in the lifetime of the boys, he had never taken them to the peak. Later in the summer he wanted to build a catch pen close to the peak and build another road. Here the trucks could come in and pick up cattle in the fall for market, saving driving the cattle to the headquarters and maybe keeping a few more pounds on the steers.

It was pitch dark when Bill got back to the house. The light in the bunkhouse was on. He knew Grandpa would be bullshitting with the cowboys. He slept in the bunkhouse after eating with the family. Inside the house he looked into the boys' room. They slept soundly, their room a mess as usual. He did not look into Frank's room. He did not feel pain about not loving the boy. This he accepted, but he did feel pain at who the boy was.

Mary was in bed reading when he walked in. She smiled as he sat down in the chair and pulled off his boots. Bill loved his wife dearly. There had been times before the war he did not know if he loved her, but during the war it was her letters that carried him through the endless days of battle and fatigue. Bill undressed and fell into bed beside his wife. He was too tired to take a shower and soon was snoring loudly in deep sleep.

Mary lay her book down and looked at the form of her sleeping husband. He was a good man and in their youth they had had a very passionate relationship. Now he was more like an old friend; working, the children and the war had taken the passion away, but it had never diminshed the warmth she felt for Bill. There had been times she wished he had married a doctor or a lawyer, not some simple rancher, but these thoughts had passed.

Coming from Boston one summer to visit a friend in Santa Fe, she had been enthralled by the West. She had met Bill in a grocery store. He was walking bowlegged with cowboy boots and a large hat, chewing tobacco sticking out of his back pocket as she stood by the vegetables in her tailored skirt and matching top, feeling very vogue and wild. The next thing she knew she was dancing in a cowboy bar and three months later she was married and walking around in Levis and cowboy boots and loving every minute of it. Mary bent over and kissed Bill's forehead and turned off the light. Life is strange, she thought, life is very strange. One just never really knows what each day will bring.

In the next room little Frank lay, his eyes wide open staring into the darkness. Around him the house creaked and groaned as he silently placed his thumb in his mouth. Slowly the forms between his eyes began to dance, they were dark men and on their faces was colored paint. Their song came to his ears as he lay watching and listening to the visions, but he did not move or smile.

CHAPTER 2
FRANK SPEAKS

Mary stood by the horse corrals and looked out to where her husband and the two eldest boys were working in the alfalfa field. She ran her hands through her hair and smiled to herself. I wonder where the last ten years have gone? It was as though today was the first time in ten years she had really seen Brad and Joe. Brad was eighteen now. A tall, slim striking young man. He was a good boy, and a good worker but she knew he was not a man like his father. She knew Brad did not want to stay on the ranch. For the past two years he had talked about a legal career. He wanted to go to California and attend shcool. Bill did not take it seriously. Telling Mary, "he will outgrow it, down deep he loves the land like I do and one day he will see this is his life."

But recently Mary could see the concern in Bill's eyes as he slowly realized Brad did truly wish to go to law school. Mary knew this hurt Bill deeply. Bill could not understand how any person would wish to do something else besides be a rancher. There was no life besides being out on the ranch. No feeling like the wind blowing across your face or the feel of a horse under you as you chased a calf or herded the cattle. There was nothing that could compare with the freedom and the openness of the outdoors.

Mary had tried many different times to talk to her husband about Brad. But no matter what she said or how she said it, Bill would not accept the fact. "No," he would finally say in disgust, "he is just a boy and doesn't know what he wants yet, he will see. I've worked my whole life to keep this ranch. Just like my father and his father before him."

She and Brad talked often about his dream. He read law books and flipped through Newsweek and Time magazine to the law sections, devouring new cases and new laws. He wanted to be a corporate lawyer. He wanted a nice house in the city and a new car. "Mom," he would say, "Dad just doesn't understand there is more to life than a ranch."

Bill did not know but within the past two weeks Brad had received a full scholarship to U.C.L.A. Neither Brad nor his mother could tell Bill — both knew it would hurt him deeply.

Over the years Bill had showered his love on Brad and Joe. Taking them with him on all things to do with the ranch. They were put into Future Farmers. They entered sheep and calves in all the state fairs. They rode in the rodeo every summer and had the best saddles and tack for their horses. Bill could look at the ranch and see his father working his life away and he could also see his life passing with the land. There was nothing else for his sons to do but carry on the ranch.

Mary also knew Joe would not stay on the ranch. Joe was sixteen, but from the time he was ten he had been a rebellious child. Unlike Brad who had never been in trouble, Joe was constantly being kicked out of school for fighting or general hell-raising. Unlike Brad, Joe had no qualms about his feelings for the ranch. He and his father had several bitter arguments. Joe hated the ranch. He hated the work and the mud and the cow shit on his clothes. He hated driving a tractor and working after school and on the weekends. He also hated little cowboy girls who talked about horses and the state fair queen. Joe liked the city. He liked hanging out with the guys in town and chasing the town girls. He could talk to his mother about it. Mary, having been raised in Boston, knew how her son felt. But she feared in her heart what the effect would be on Bill when the boys left.

Mary turned toward the house. The ranch had not been quite the same since Grandpa died, bless his good soul. Grandpa had been a mediator between the boys and Bill. A silent voice that could communicate both sides. Even Grandpa had seen the boys did not wish to stay on the ranch. It had hurt him at first but he accepted it. "Man has to be what he has to be, Mary," he would say. "It's a big world out there. Bill is just going to have to accept it and go on. Hell, you two are not getting any younger, you could sell this place and travel around the world until you die." With this Grandpa had bowed his head. "Lisa always wanted us to take some time and go places. She had travel brochures and books about Greece and Spain, Italy. But I would never take the time. Man should do more than just work his life away. Man should see the world. Those two boys are good boys, but the are not ranching people. It's too bad, but it's Frank who knows the land."

Mary walked into the kitchen and lying on the kitchen table were several dark arrow points. She smiled and picked them up. Frank had put them there. Poor Frank, she thought. Of all the boys, she knew she loved Frank the most. Poor tiny Frank. But it was funny, for his size he had never been sick in his life. He was small, but he was not frail. His energy was endless. Still, he was so alone. After ten years he still had never spoken a word. His father or the other boys never took him out to work, and to Mary it seemed like Bill did not even acknowledge his presence. But Frank with his large brown eyes seemed oblivious to it all. Mary knew there was more to Frank than people saw. He seemed to take into his eyes all that was around him. Weighing sounds and voices. It was as though Frank was a part of the land around them. Silent and seeminly uncaring. Mary felt he communicated with the earth and was beyond what man called communication with words. He still had never shown any form of love or emotion to Mary. He had never hugged or kissed her.

But he brought her things he found on the ranch. When he was eight, Frank had started to go out on the ranch alone. Returning from town one afternoon, Mary had gone into a panic when she could not find Frank. She had searched and searched until dark and was sitting on the porch on the verge of tears when Frank had walked back to the house. She had run to him and held him and smoothed his ruffled hair. Frank had just stood and held out his hand palm up and given Mary a small red arrowhead. And for the first time Mary knew the boy felt.

From that day on, Mary would pack the boy a small lunch every day the weather was nice, and Frank would go out onto the ranch, a small silent form that walked the sand washes and climbed the rocky bluffs. He explored the Indian ruins and old rock Mexican homesteader shacks. He poked through the old Ortiz hacienda. Mary would watch him as he disappeared from view. A tiny, alone figure moving slowly across the land, almost invisible, so at one with the land was he. He did not walk over the earth, he walked with the land. His large brown eyes picked up the scampering of rabbits and the small trails of black beetles. He could reach out and touch the circling hawks and crows. The land and the animals accepted him. There was no hate in his body, no bad will. He was a walking, moving form of true life. Life not encumbered by love or hate, wishes or desires. He saw what was around him as what it was, not as what he wanted it to be.

Mary had taken Frank to a doctor in town. He had been poked and examined, tested and probed. After all the tests, the psychologist and the doctors all told Mary he was a healthy boy. He was not simple or insane, he just did not speak. There were cases like his recorded where one day the person would just begin to speak as if nothing had ever been wrong.

Mary had decided not to send the boy to school, but she spent hours showing him the alphabet and letters and words with flash cards. She knew Frank could read. One afternoon she had found an old book on cowboys that belonged to Joe left on the table. From that day on Mary bought the boy books. He would sit in his room devouring the books. He read everything, but he especially liked books about Indians and the early West, and he read far beyond the normal mind of a young boy.

Looking at Frank it was as though he was an old man in a boy's body. His eyes held and captivated a person, enough so most people could not look at his gaze for long. It was like his eyes bore into your soul, pulling out all your strength and weakness. They deciphered your being leaving nothing but a hollowness inside.

Frank was eleven when one afternoon she saw him ride by on

a horse. The horse was saddled and bridled and Frank had adjusted the stirrups to fit his small legs. No one had ever taught him to ride, taught him to saddle a horse. But there he was riding like an old pro. After dinner that night she told Bill and Bill had only looked at her and spoke, "I'll be damned, that boy is sure a strange one."

Riding the horse, Frank poked deeper and deeper into the corners of the ranch. By twelve he knew the ranch better than even his father. He knew hidden caves and old Indian campsites. He knew where the coyotes had their babies and where the hawks nested. His room was filled with arrowhheads and old broken pieces of purple glass. There was pottery and mule bones and horse skulls. Mary standing in his room when he was gone would feel as though she was standing in a time chamber or a museum. Here was the unwritten history of the land around her.

What Mary or the boys or Bill did not know was that Frank was never alone. It was the shadows that kept him silent. The strange forms and images that came to his eyes, dancing and weaving spells over his mind. They were his friends and his family. He could see them everywhere and when he could not see them he could feel them. They called to him and kept him warm inside. Frank as he grew older began to understand the forms were ghosts — images of time past.

When Frank was eight, he had his first real vision that was not a mere swift passage through his mind. Standing at the bottom of a slowly falling sand and clay hillside by the old church, Indian ruins and Mexican shack, there had been a man. A tall thin man and he was riding a horse, and behind him were three mules. The mules had on large packs and seemed to be tired from the weight. The man was dirty and tired and in his hand he held a rifle. His eyes darted from the cliff to the land behind him. Frank had stood and looked at the form and the form turned and looked down at him and a smile had spread across the man's face and he waved. With the wave he vanished into the air.

Frank stood and looked at the empty space for several moments. In his mind he knew that the form at one time had been alive. At one time he had ridden across this land and he knew that now the man was going to another life. Walking through the Indian ruins, Frank could see the Indians and he could see the ruin as it was when the Indians were alive. There were no falling crumbling walls. No old homes with pinon trees and cedar trees growing from their floors. There were women and children and young braves breaking horses. There were old men sitting in small groups talking about being young. Frank would pick up broken pottery and arrow points and he could feel the life that lived and breathed inside them. He could see the hands of the people who made them and he knew he was a part of life and time.

At times sitting on top of a high bluff or mesa, Frank would see the Spanish soldiers as they rode across the land. The armor and metal helmets reflecting the sun as it bore down on them. And by the old church one afternoon he saw a small round fat man with a long brown robe. The priest had waved to Frank and Frank waved back. Standing in the homesteader's shack he could hear babies cry and feel the soft touch of a woman around him.

But Frank could not formulate into words the things that he saw. Sitting at home with his mother he had tried several times but there was no sound that emitted from his mouth, nothing that would bring the visions and images around him into words. So he lived with his timeless friends and his feelings, and he came to know the land around him and the deep sense of time and space that came with the knowledge.

Mary looked around the kitchen and took a deep breath. It was time to start dinner. The boys would be done soon and would be hungry as bears.

Brad worked in the field throwing the large alfalfa bales onto the flatbed trailer being pulled by the tractor. His father drove the tractor, too old now to throw many bales. Brad did not understand how his father continued each day working so hard. Already Bill's back hurt and his hands were beginning to twist and knot from all the abuse during the years. Brad wished he could talk to his father. Tell him how he loved him and tell him how much he appreciated all he had done for him, but over the past year ever since Brad had told his father he wanted to be a lawyer, they had not been able to talk. He knew his father loved him deeply, but he also knew his father would never accept the fact that Brad did not want to stay on the ranch. After school was out in a few weeks, Brad would pack his suitcase and go to California. He had already tried to sit down and write a letter to his father, telling him how he felt, telling him why he had to go — but he could never start the letter. His father seemed like a stranger to him. They were so different. It hurt Brad deeply, but there was nothing he could do. He knew if he stayed on the ranch he would forever wonder what would have happened to his life if he had gone to California and law school. He would miss it all, he knew — miss the smell of fresh cut hay, miss his brother and mother, miss his father, but he was almost a man and there was a world for him that was not here. He did not want to be a rancher. He hoped Joe in a few years might want to stay on the ranch. They had talked about it a lot in their room.

"Dad just doesn't understand," Joe would say. "To him there is nothing else but stinking cows and working all day. I don't want to grow up and be doubled over in pain when I'm fifty. I want to see the world. I want nice clothes and nice clean city women."

To Brad, Joe was a very superficial person. Brad was far deeper and more concerned with other people's feelings than Joe. "If Frank wasn't such a simple fucker, we would both be off the hook," Joe spoke. "Hell, he has been in more places on this piece of shit ranch than any of us."

Brad frowned. "Frank is different, that's all, Joe. He's not simple."

Joe laughed,. "Collecting all that Indians stuff and all those old bones. He give me the creeps with those brown eyes of his. It's like he was a space man or something. A flying saucer landed here and instead of his being born, they just dropped him at the house one day."

"Joe, you're fucked in your head," Brad mumbled. "The only thing you think about is fucking and getting in trouble in school."

Joe grinned. "Well, what the hell? Could be worse things. If you would get a girlfriend and try a little fucking you might see more to the world than wanting to be some goddamn lawyer out in California."

Brad looked at his brother, "Sometimes I worry about you. It's not Frank who's the strange one."

Bill stopped the tractor and climbed down to the ground slowly. Jesus, his back hurt. He remembered the words of his father: Ranching doesn't do anything but break your back and shorten your life. He walked towards his two sons. Brad would change his mind, he knew he would. He might go to California for a while, but once out there, trapped in some big city, he would find out how much he missed the ranch and the freedom. "Let's go eat, boys," he spoke, "Your mother should have dinner ready by now. Then we can get back and get the rest of these bales in."

Mary and Bill and the two boys ate dinner slowly. "Where do you suppose Frank is," Joe said. Mary shook her head, "Never can tell. As long as he's back by dark."

Frank stood by the Mexican homesteader's shack and sweat rolled down his brow. There were six of them. Young wild looking Indians riding painted, frothing horses. They charged in around him and shot a Mexican man leaving the house. Then dismounting they dragged the screaming terrified woman out of the house and with four men holding her naked body to the ground, took turns on top of her. Her screams filled his ears as her blood flowed onto the ground. Soon the woman was motionless and the braves stood and spit on her dead form. Then they ran into the house and dragged out two children. They children they tied with ropes and remounting their horses they dragged the small bodies through the pinon and cedar trees until they were like bundles of blood-soaked rags. Frank held his brow and shut his eyes, trying to stop the sights around him, but they woud not stop. And with his hands to his temples, he opened his mouth and a deep piercing scream split the air. He turned and mounting his horse and galloped the horse back towards the house, screaming, "MOTHER! MOTHER! Make them go away!"

It was several miles back to the house. Frank rode oblivious to all around him. When he reached the house, Bill and the boys were in the workshop. Frank burst into the kitchen. Mary was doing the dishes and Frank ran to her and buried his head into her side and wrapped his small arms around her waist. And in between deep sobs he spoke, "Mother, mother, make them go away, make them stop," and then a deep shudder spread through his body and in one last gasp he muttered into his mother's side, "I love you, Mother, I love you."

Mary held her sobbing son and the words were like spring rain coming to the land. She stroked the hair of the boy and felt his wet tears go through her dress. "Frank, my little Frank, it's okay, dear one, everything is going to be okay." And they stood arm in arm as the silence slowly drifted away.

From that day, Frank spoke. Bill and Mary and the boys were amazed at what he knew. He spoke as though he had never been silent for twelve years. He knew about T.V. and the radio. He knew the trees and the birds by name. But was still a silent boy. He still kept apart from Bill and the boys, only saying a few remarks during any conversation. And he still went out alone with the land, but he did not venture back to the homesteader's ruin nor did he tell anybody of his visions around the ranch.

CHAPTER 3
THE PARTINGS

Brad stepped up to the bus driver and held out his ticket. The driver smiled faintly and punched the slip for him. "L.A." he spoke, "That's a long way, young man." Brad smiled, although he did not feel like smiling, and stepped into the bus. Taking a deep breath he walked to the back row of seats and sat down. He had told his parents he was spending the weekend with some friends and packed a small suitcase with some clothes. They would not know he was gone for several days. He did not leave them a letter. The words had never come but he would call them from California. He felt confused, but he also felt good. He had never been out of the state, never seen the ocean or girls wearing bikinis. He was pulled to the big city the way his ancestors had been pulled to the West.

The bus lurched to a start and slowly made its way out of Santa Fe. Gaining speed outside of town, Brad could see the back side of the mountain where the Ortiz gold mine was and on the other side he knew his father and brother were working on a fence and his mother would be doing laundry. Frank would be out somewhere picking at the rocks and the cattle would be walking slowly, eating the grass. A small tear came to his eye and he looked around to see that nobody was watching. "Goodbye," he spoke to the passing mountain, "goodbye."

Bill and Joe stood back and looked down the quarter mile stretch of fence they had just finished. Bill liked looking at new fence. It was something tangible that one saw completion in when the work was done. "That fence will be there long after I'm dead and gone," Bill said.

Joe sat down, "I hope so. I'd hate to make that thing again."

Bill laughed. He remembered when he was a kid and how he hated to work at times. His father would have to keep kicking him along. Do this Bill, now do this Bill. He had wanted to leave the ranch when he was young, tired of the endless work. Tired of the flies in the summer and the cold in the winter. But when he met Mary that had all changed. With Mary there was no desire to go any place. She was adventure enough. Bill sat down beside his son and opened up his lunch box. "Where's your lunch?" he asked Joe. Joe stood. "It's in the truck. I'll go get it."

Bill sat eating his sandwich and sipping hot coffee and thought about his wife. He would never forget the first time he saw her in that grocery store. It was as though everything around her disappeared and all he could see was her slim figure and her blonde hair. He barely remembered walking up to her and to this day didn't know why she came with him dancing or why she married him. She, with her college degree and her fine back east upbringing. But she was still with him. Three children and nineteen years later. She was a fine loving woman, a fact in his life he would never regret. Joe came back with his lunch box and sat down. Around them the wind skipped over the pinon trees and several mountain jays squawked.

Joe dug into his lunch box. One day I won't eat my lunch out of a box, he said to himself. I'll eat in the finest restaurants and waiters will bring me my food.

Lunch over, Bill and his son stood and Bill turned and looked at Joe. "One day you will love this land like I do, son," he spoke. "You will look out here and you will see your grandfather and me and remember all the things you hate now as fond memories." Joe looked away from his father and thought, no, Dad, I will never miss this place, never in my life.

Mary sat out in the yard and she knew Brad was on his way to California. She had seen it in his eyes the day before when he was telling her he was going into town for the weekend. She had wanted to reach out and hold him close to her and tell him he must follow his dreams, but she could not. There were so many things she wanted to tell him, but there had been no words. She only stood and watched him pack his small bag and knew he would be on the bus, off to find his dreams, far away in another state. She did not cry when he left in the morning. She did not cry until late in the afternoon when she went to his room and looked at the marks of time — old airplane models, ribbons from state fairs, and his letter jacket. They grew so quickly and were gone — all the time, all the years and tears, all the heartache and then they were gone. Mary left the room and felt cold and tired.

Monday evening when the phone rang Bill knew it was Brad and he knew Brad was in California. "I'm sorry, Dad," Brad stammered. Bill held the phone loosely in his weatherbeaten hands and answered softly, "Everybody's got to do what he's got to do, son. I'll get your mother on the phone." And Bill called Mary.

After that Bill did not talk about Brad. On the outside to his friends he seemed normal. But inside he carried a deep burning scar, and with time and thought, he disinherited his eldest son. He could not believe that any career was better than the ranch. The ranch was tradition, it was history. It had been in the family for over one hundred years. Any man who would do this was beyond help and a selfish and heartless man. Bill would never tell Mary about this, but Mary without his words knew that Brad was forever shut out of his father's life. With this Bill went out of his way to be with Joe. Joe would not speak of his desires about life. He knew that when the time came, he would have to leave like Brad.

But with all of this, Bill still did not pay any attention to Frank. There had been so many years of separation that Bill could not reach out to the boy even when he wished to at times. Frank was like a love he couldn't have and therefore should be forgotten.

Frank was a normal twelve-year-old in many respects but he remained a loner. He would be going to school after the summer, only one grade behind what should have been his normal class. But mostly Frank went out onto the ranch alone to be with the ghosts, and he began to truly see the land around him. He could see where erosion should be checked. He could look out at the pastures and know it was time to move the cattle. He started to pick the wild grasses and at night he looked them up in the encyclopedia and read all about them. He dug sample holes all over the ranch, checking the soil and the roots of the grass, and by looking at slopes and drainage areas he calculated where windmills could be placed so the cattle would not have to walk so far, thus keeping on the needed pounds for market. He looked and saw where hillsides that were now bare could be planted with wild grasses for feed.

Beyond the ranch, life had no interest for Frank. He did not bother with T.V. or listen to the radio. He did not ever get asked to parties with other children or wish to be in the state fair or the rodeo. Even when he was somewhere with his parents and there were other children, he did not run around and play but stayed with the adults. It was not that he was not able, it was just that he did not want to.

On his thirteenth birthday after blowing out the candles, his mother looked at him smiling and said, "What do you want to be Frank?" And without hesitation or thought and having never asked himself the question, Frank blurted out, "An old-time cowboy."

Bill's head had jerked back and he looked closely at Frank and noticed for the first time the boy was beginning to build up. His shoulders were broader and his cheeks that had been hollow for so long were now beginning to fill in. He was no longer frail and weak looking. Joe sat waiting for the cake and ice cream and dreaming about one more year of high school and his escape from the ranch.

That night lying in bed Bill talked to his wife in the darkness. "Can you imagine that Frank saying he wanted to be a cowboy?" Mary could hear a glimmer of hope in Bill's voice. "He sure has grown up this last year. You'd hardly ever know he was once so small and frail and strange." Mary reached over and touched her husband's hand. "He'll make a fine cowboy, Bill, the best in the area. His true mother is the land."

Frank lay in bed that night and the visions returned. He could see cowboys riding on the ranch and he saw his grandfather when he was a young man. He had on chaps and a leather vest and a large white droopy cowboy hat. His horse was frothing at the mouth as grandfather chased down a runaway calf. That is what Frank wanted. He wanted the ranch to be a real ranch. No pickup trucks or tractors. He would have horses and wagons, no tractors. He would only grow wild grasses. And there would be cattle. A mother cow operation. He would breed his cows and sell his calves and all the work would be done on horseback. His ranch would be like the West used to be. As he had seen for himself. It would be like the land should be — free and natural.

After only one year of high school, Frank knew he did not like the city world. It made him feel nervous and alone. He did not like the loud seemingly senseless chatter of all the kids, not the cars and trucks that filled the streets. Everybody was more interested in what they looked like or if their clothes were in style. The best part of school and town was getting on the bus and being let out back on the ranch. There was only sanity on the land and the touch of the earth and the wind.

CHAPTER 4
THE SPEAR POINT

Bill sat in the living room and stared outside through the window. He could not remember when the snowflakes had been this large. Already the snow was two feet deep. If it kept up like this, by morning it would be at least five feet deep. Bill did not think about the cows that would be trapped by the snow. He only gazed out upon the snow and tried to stop the ache that was in his heart. It had already been fourteen months but the passage of time did nothing to quell the pain that surrounded him.

Everything was going so well. The ranch had shown a good profit for two years. The weather had been cooperative for once. There was just the right amount of snow in the late winter to get the grass growing, and the springtime had been wet and warm. And then Joe was killed. Out one night with some friends they had been drinking beer and driven the car into a power pole. All four of the boys were dead instantly. Bill was sitting at home reading some mail. Mary was taking a bath and Frank had been stitching up a saddle that had been torn when the telephone rang. The police told Bill he had to come to the hospital and identify his son.

Bill did not tell Mary or Frank why he was leaving. The only thing recognizable about Joe were his boots. Driving back to the ranch Bill did not cry or feel anything. There was no world, no night, no drone of the truck tires. There was only emptiness that encompassed his entire body. When Mary heard the news she cried all night. There was nothing anybody could do for her but leave her alone with her agony.

Frank went out onto the porch and sat down on the old swing. Beside him sat the image of his grandfather and beside his grandfather appeared the image of his father, and walking by the horse corrals Frank could see Joe. And Frank began to cry. Large deep tears wracked his body and the tears streamed down his face. But just as suddenly as the crying had started it stopped and Frank stood and walked out onto the yard. Standing there he knew he would be the only hope for the ranch. And looking up at the stars surrounded by the cottonwoods his grandfather's mother had planted, he vowed he would forever be on the ranch. There would never be one piece of this land used for anything but a cattle ranch.

Going back inside the house he walked up to his father who was sitting in a chair staring blankly at the wall, and putting his hand on his father's shoulder he spoke, "The land will always be in our family." And he walked to his room and lay on his bed, eyes open and peering into the darkness.

Bill stood and walked to the kitchen and the snow was still falling outside. "God, I wish it would go away," he mumbled. There were brief periods of time when Bill did not ache over Joe. Periods of time where there was no pain or grief. Time when he could remember little things about Joe that made him happy. He did not think about the fact that Joe was a hell-raiser and did not like the ranch. But these moments never lasted long before the aches and emptiness returned.

When Brad came back for the funeral, he was a tall handsome man of twenty. His grades had been excellent and he already had offers from several major law firms. The first thing Bill thought at seeing his son was, he is no longer a cowboy. Brad wore slacks and a light cotton shirt and loafers. He was deeply tanned and in excellent shape. Upon seeing Brad, Bill knew his son would never take over the ranch, but try as he might, he could not see in Frank a man of the strength or stamina needed to run the ranch. When Brad left to go back to California, Bill was relieved to see him go. With him gone it was just one more ache he did not have to endure.

Bill opened the refrigerator door and looked inside, but he knew he was not hungry, and he closed the door slowly and walked back to his chair by the window. The war had not been this way. It was easy to get over the pain of the war, or it seemed to have been. But it was different, he supposed. There had been Mary and the two boys and Grandfather. Even the touch of Mary did not warm him now, and he knew that his feelings hurt Mary. She was much stronger than he. She did not fall into depths of depression and show everybody her pain. Bill knew there was a separation between them now. The longer he felt the pain, the more inadequate Mary would feel. "Damn cows are going to be buried to their shoulders," he spoke, trying to change his thoughts. But no matter what he thought or did, the sadness over his son was like an invisible dark cloud that traveled with him. After all the years of keeping the ranch together, dreaming and hoping both Brad and Joe would stay on the land, Bill no longer had the desire to keep the ranch. He thought maybe if he sold the place, he and Mary would move and start a completely new life. A life not filled with mementos of time, a life where there were no memories. A life where he could get up in the morning and look out and see things fresh and alive, not filled with ghosts.

Bill did not think about Frank often. Before Joe's death there was a period of time where Bill began to watch Frank closely. Frank indeed did have a feel for the land and the animals. But even with his new feelings, Bill could not reach out and hold his son. He could not tell him he loved him and cared for him deeply because inside himself he really did not know if he did or not. But since Joe's death, Bill as before was seldom conscious of Frank's presence. He did not notice the extra work Frank did. Around the house the ranch had never been in better shape. All the tools and gear were in a specific place and taken care of. Alfalfa bales were catalogued and a count kept. There was no wire thrown around or garbage. The ranch was impeccable. All the horse stalls and runs were cleaner than they had ever been. Frank did the work of three men. But even though his father did not notice, the two cowboys working the ranch began to notice and began to like the young man who was strangely silent. One of the old cowboys, a man in his fifties who had worked ranches all over the West told his friend, ''That young buck sure knows his shit and never wastes any words either.'' His friend nodded his head, 'Has to be a crazy bastard just like us to want to keep this place going. This modern day ranching is a lot of work for no pay.''

But even with all of the work, Bill was oblivious to Frank. It was as though gremlins came out with the night and did all the work. Mary did not bother to tell Bill how selfish he was being. There was no need. He would not be able to push the pain away or comprehend the long-range effects of his actions. But although it hurt Mary to see Bill shun Frank, it did not seem to bother Frank. Having never felt his father's love, he did not really miss it.

All Frank could see was the ranch and the responsibility he would receive when it was truly his. For now all his work and time was but a beginning when he would have the complete say-so about the ranch.

The next morning Frank did not go to school, which he did not mind, as in his thoughts he had already decided he was going to run the ranch. There was no need for the education he was receiving. Although he did get good grades it was only from the constant prodding by his mother. Frank had his father's horse and his own saddled and ready to go before the sun came up. He grained them well to help endure the cold day. Going back in the house his father was drinking coffee and Mary was cooking breakfast. ''Horses are ready, Dad,'' Frank spoke smiling. ''The storm has broken.'' Across the way the two cowboys rustled around in the bunkhouse knowing they would be looking for cows this day. Bill nodded his head and sipped his coffee. Frank, looking at his father, noticed the large dark circles under his eyes, but instead of feeling sad for his father, he felt a small thread of anger — but he said nothing.

After breakfast and sitting in the bunkhouse with the cowboys, it was decided George and Rooster would ride north and circle back east along several ridge lines. These ridges made good wind breaks, and if the men were lucky the cattle would head for these and would not have been caught out in the open plains by the storm. Frank and his father would ride down the bottom of the ridge that ran off the mesa top and circle out and around the old Mexican ruin and the church. If there was nothing there, they would ride towards the box canyon and then back to the house.

Riding was tough in the snow but there was enough wind that there were alleyways in the drifts that the horses could walk through. Frank rode bundled up with warm clothes and looked out over the snow-covered land. Everything seemed so peaceful and pure after a snow. It was strange to Frank how something so beautiful at times could be so deadly. He had seen more than one cow in his lifetime standing frozen to death caught in the deep snow. Frank felt invigorated riding. What with school he did not get out as much as he liked to. There was only Saturday and Sunday to ride and see the ranch. But he only had two more years of school and he could be on the ranch every day of his life. As they rode farther out away from the house, the wind began to kick up and he and his father wrapped their long scarves around their faces leaving only their eyes exposed under the drooping cowboy hats. His father had spoken little as they were riding. Gazing out into the distance trying to spot the black spots of the angus cattle. A storm like this and a man could be wiped out for years. But Frank knew his father was not worried about this. Deep in his heart Frank felt the distance his father now had from the ranch.

The wind was blowing, a gale kicking the fresh snow into the air and making it like small cutting razors that cut into the eyes of the horses and stung what ever skin became exposed on Bill and Frank. They were both chilled to the bone and when they dismounted by the old Mexican ruin, they were ready for lunch and a hot cup of coffee from the thermos. Bill took the horses and tied them on the downwind side of the old rock house. Frank stood outside remembering the ghosts when he was a boy. He did not like to come to this place. It was not a good place and he could smell the death, but this day he did not see the ghosts. Both men gathered an armful of dead wood and going inside where a corner of the room was protected from the wind, they built a blazing fire.

"How would you have liked to live in this house like those Mexicans?" Bill asked. "Would have made winter a lot different than what we know."

Frank felt ill-at-ease sitting in the old house and answered in a low voice, "I'm satisfied to be alive now."

Bill poured two cups of coffee and handed one to Frank who sat down by the fire. Slowly the warmth spread through his body and within a few minutes after sipping the coffee and eating a sandwich, he felt normal again. Looking at the rock walls around him, Frank shook his head. "These people worked hard to make this house."

Bill agreed. "It was different times then, boy. They worked hard every day. Everything was toil — hauling water, eating, fighting Indians and bandits, trying to make a small living off of this hard land. I always wondered what happened here," Bill continued, "What made these people after so much work just pull up and move away. Its's like the earth just swallowed them up."

Frank wanted to tell his father he knew what happened. He wanted to tell him he had seen it with his own eyes. But he knew his father would only laugh or think Frank was strange. But he had seen it. Seen the massacre as he had seen the man with the mules on the ridge above the old house and as he had seen the Indians down in the village at times and the Spaniards riding across the mesa heading for the old Ortiz hacienda. He wanted to tell his father about the land and maybe his father would lose his pain and agony and once again come back to what Frank knew he loved most in life, this ranch. But there were no words, just the comment, "I don't know. I wonder if some man some day will be sitting by our house wondering the same thing about it."

Bill laughed. "Fuckin' time doesn't wait for anybody, I suppose. It's hard to figure, everything seems so permanent and solid, but when it all comes right down to it, there is nothing permanent and solid. There is just every day, one day at a time." After Bill spoke, the sudden and deep impact of his words settled into his heart. That was it — he had to take every day one at a time, that was how simple it was. Frank looked at his father and he could see the deep ache come off his face and he knew that his father was back with the world.

Bill sat silent for a few minutes and then he spoke, "When your grandfather was a little boy, they didn't live much different than this. It's only in the past fifty or sixty years life has started to become easier for ranchers. Think if all the work we save by using gas heat alone." Bill stood up and walked across the small room to go out and gather another armful of wood. As he walked, his boot heel caught on something. Stepping back and lookng down he could see a small black point sticking from the ground, and he bent over and with his pocket knife dug around the point. Within a few moments he held a six-inch spear point in his hand. "Well, I'll be damned," he spoke, "never seen a spear point like this one. It has a hole drilled through the base of it." With that he stood up and looking at Frank, tossed the spear point to him. Before Frank had caught the point, his father was turned and outside the old door jamb.

When the point landed in Frank's hands, wave after wave of feeling rushed over him. And with the feeling, for the first time Frank felt a great aloneness enter his heart. Looking at the point it seemed like the point was a living, breathing heart, lying pulsating in his hands. There was everything in the world in the point and more. There were birds and coyotes and deer and the wind. Frank looked at the flickering flames from the fire dancing across the gleaming surface of the point and before his eyes he could see a young brave sitting by a small fire holding this same point, and he felt deep rolling torrents of love flow though his body. Looking deep into the eyes of the Indian he knew this man made this point in his hands for a young maiden who was far from his side. And Frank could feel the longing and loneliness sweep across the face of time. The Indian took the point and holding his two hands together raised the point to the heavens and began to sing.

After the song was finished the vision disappeared, and swimming in the center of the point the face of a blond-haired girl appeared. She was the most beautiful girl Frank had ever seen and she was smiling. Her small delicate lips moved and she spoke, "Frank, Frank I love you."

When Bill came back into the ruin he looked at Frank and spoke. "Looks like you've seen a ghost, are you okay?"

Frank took a deep breath and nodded his head, "I'm fine, Dad, I just felt a little funny for a moment." He took the spear point and put it in his jacket pocket and watched as the wood his father brought in slowly caught fire.

A short while later they kicked the fire out and remounted their horses and rode towards the box canyon. At times in a storm if there was a smart lead cow, the cattle could head for the safety of the box canyon. Frank and Joe had torn down part of an old rock wall that had been built across the mouth of the canyon one summer, making a large entrance for the cattle. They rode and Frank trailed behind his father. He could still see glimpses of the girl in his mind. Frank was not conscious of being in front of the box canyon when his father spoke. "No cattle here. Guess Rooster and George must've found them. We can head for home and get out of this cold." Frank's father started to ride off, but Frank did not move. There before him lying on the ground was an Indian. The mangled pile of flesh and bone was not recognizable as a human being, but Frank knew it was an Indian. Kicking his horse Frank left the spot to catch up with his father and try to leave the ghosts behind him.

Back at the ranch headquarters George and Rooster were in the barn feeding their horses when Bill and Frank rode in. Rooster spit a gob of tobacco out onto the ground. "Cattle's all over by the bluffs. They're fine, but we should haul out some hay for them in the morning."

That night lying in bed, Frank held the point in his hands and turned it slowly. As he turned the point a faint image of a girl's face appeared before his eyes. She was a beautiful girl. Her eyes were blue. Her blonde hair fell gently down and around her face. She smiled at Frank and whispered, "I love you, Frank, I love you with all my life." Frank rose from the bed and opening his dresser drawer he placed the point in the back of the drawer and closed it slowly. But lying in bed with the lights out he could not stop the vision of the blonde girl appearing from the darkness.

Bill lay in bed and gently he lay his arm across Mary. "Mary," he spoke in a whisper, "I'll never forget Joe and there will always be an ache in my heart, but it's okay now, my love, it's okay." Mary placed her hand on her husband's hand and was silent. Only their steady even breathing echoed throughout the room.

CHAPTER 5
THE WILL

Frank helped his mother into the pickup truck. Looking at her she seemed much older than her sixty years. Her once blonde hair was now a pale white and her blue eyes that seemed so full of life were dull and tired. It has been a nice funeral. Brad had flown in and spent the last week on the ranch. He and Frank had never talked as much as they did. They talked about Bill mostly and mother, but very little about the ranch. The will would be read in the morning and whatever conversation about the ranch would wait until then.

Bill died doing what he loved best — riding his horse over the ranch. For the past five years the doctors had told him to slow down, take it easier. He and Mary had taken several vacations. One to Hawaii, three weeks in Europe. Mary loved the trips dearly but after a week Bill would be restless and calling Frank every day asking if there was any emergency. Frank only laughed telling his father, "It's okay, Dad, nothing can happen that I can't handle."

Bill had risen early one morning and saddled his horse. It was early spring and the sun was beginning to rise above the land. Bill knew the sun would feel good on his old bones by noon. There was nothing he really had to do. Frank did everything well. He just wanted to ride and be alone for the day. Riding he pointed his horse towards Devil's Peak. It had been years since he had been there, but today a strange compulsion came over him. By ten o'clock the day was warm and the new life of spring was all around him. It would a good year for the gamma grass, Bill thought. The winter had been mild and there were very few cows lost which might make the ranch show a good profit. The past years had not been great for money but they had not been bad. To this day Bill had never once had to go to the bank and borrow money on the land. In this fact he was very proud. He spent hours preaching to Frank, "Never let the fucking bank touch the deeds. No matter how they smile or shake your hand, they'll cut your throat in a minute."

Bill rode and it was strange but for the first time in ages he thought about his father and he began to remember little things he and his father had done when he was a boy. And he thought about Brad and he had a strange desire to turn his horse around and ride back to the house and call Brad and tell him it was okay, okay to want to live your own life. Okay to not want to stay on the land. Brad was doing well in California. He had a good law business going, a fine wife with two small children, and a home. A sudden wave of sadness wept over Bill thinking about Brad. He would call him tonight and tell him he was sorry for being so bitter over the years. "You're becoming an old man," Bill chuckled, "life seems different and things one held important lose their importance. The importance is to live and try not to hurt anybody." Bill took a deep breath and savored the feel of the spring air. Life, I love you so, he thought.

Dismounting his horse by Devil's Peak, Bill felt tired. He was tired a lot these days. There was no spring in his step. He felt in his mind he could still do the things he did when he was a young man and oftentimes sitting in his chair dozing he would dream he was young, but he would wake knowing they were only dreams. Bill began to walk around the base of Devil's Peak. The pictographs on the face of the peak were ageless. He remembered when his father brought him here as a small boy and the words his father spoke. This is our legacy, Bill, we are but scratches on a rock, always trying to be more than we are, striving for a toe hold on the earth but we are in truth no greater than the smallest grain of sand. But we all leave our mark on the world, like these drawings — we all try to prove we are not mere mortals when deep down inside we know we are but a passing.

Bill walked around the corner of the peak and there before him was the horse with the small cross above it. Time had done nothing to the horse. It still ran and breathed deep the air around it, blessed by the cross above its withers. Standing looking at the horse Bill felt small and vulnerable. Life was such a quick thing, years running into years, seeming like days. He reached out with his hand and touched the rough lines of the horse and as he did so a deep pain shot through his chest and he fell, dead before he hit the ground.

Frank found him the next morning after searching all night. He picked up his father's body and lay him in the back of the pickup truck. Unsaddling the horse and putting the tack beside his father he thumped the horse which would return to the ranch headquarters by itself. Driving back Frank did not cry although he felt deeply grieved. There was never a tangible love between him and his father, not even in death could this gap be bridged.

Mary sat in the pickup truck and watched the landscape roll by on the way to the ranch. She looked over at Frank. He was a handsome man now. There was no trace that he had ever been thin. No trace that he had not spoken for so many years. He had dirty blonde hair cut short and a clean well-scrubbed looking face. Although not large, 155 pounds, he was strong and his muscles were well-defined. He looked so much like Bill when he was a young man. She looked away from Frank and thought to herself, I wish you would fall in love, my son. I wish you would find something more important than this ranch.

The next morning in town the lawyer looked out from behind his desk at Mary, Frank and Brad. The will was simple and straight to the point. Everything was left to Frank, the ranch and everything to do with the ranch. Brad received nothing. Leaving the office, Brad shook Frank's hand. "I guess he never got over the fact I didn't want to be a rancher." Frank looked into his brother's eyes and saw the deep sadness that settled there. "I'm sorry, Brad," he spoke, "I'm very sorry." That afternoon Brad flew back to California, happy to leave New Mexico.

The next morning Frank told the two cowboys working for him, Peter and Wesley, that he needed a few more hands. He was going to change a few things on the ranch. I'm going to make this ranch like an old-time ranch. From now on we will do all our work by horseback. I am going to buy several wagons for feeding in the winter. Most of this machinery is going to be sold except two pickup trucks. Alfalfa will be cut by horse and sickle and piled in stacks. All trucks coming onto the ranch will not be permitted to go any farther than the headquarters here. The cowboys were happy. It was hard to be a cowboy now. Hell, being a cowboy today was mostly running machinery and having grease on your hands. Frank looked at the two hands. "There's a ranch in Nevada that is strictly a horse operation and this is going to be the only other ranch in the West that will hang onto the old life." Within a week Frank had the tractors and machinery sold and within two weeks the harness gear for the team of horses was on its way from Colorado. Frank knew it would be rough. It was hard to make a ranch work, make ends meet. The cost of everything rose daily but it would work and his ranch would be known all over the West for being a true Western ranch.

Telling his mother about what he was doing, Mary smiled deeply looking at her son and spoke, "You were destined for this, Frank, from the time you were a little boy the land has reached out for you. It has meant more to you than anything else in your life, including me." And Frank, looking at his mother, knew this was true. There was nothing else in the world more important than this ranch.

That night sitting in his room Frank took the black obsidian spear point from his drawer. Holding it before him, he was enraptured by the magic of the point. Swimming in the center of the point he could see his father and mother when they were young. They were laughing and holding hands and then once again the vision returned of the girl with flowing blonde hair. Her image floated up out of the point and surrounded Frank. "I love you, I love you," she spoke. Frank put the point back in the drawer and lay down on his bed and for the first time in his life he felt lonely. He wanted a woman to be with him. He wanted the touch and feel of a woman's hands. He wanted to reach out and bring into his arms something that was soft and warm. And he lay staring into the ceiling bringing into his mind the image from the point and wishing love was something you could go to the store and pick out and wear like a new shirt.

By midsummer Frank had the ranch the way he wanted it. The wagons were shipped in from Colorado and he had bought two fine teams of horses. He hired six cowboys, each in their own way colorful figures. Looking at them one would wonder if it was indeed not 1880. They all wore traditional large drooping cowboy hats and very high-heeled boots. Each man had his own special pair of large rowled spurs and his set of chaps. They were all strong tough men. Each a loner, none married or thinkng of getting married. There was no room for marriage in their lives. They were called to a life that paid little for the work but it was a good life. A life outdoors with no man a true boss. If they liked the ranch they were on they stayed. If they didn't, they left. Saturday night was the traditional go-to-town-and-get-drunk night looking for loose women that hung out in the cowboy bars. But they were fair, honest men. Men that seemed to carry a deep hurt inside themselves. And to a man, they liked Frank and they liked the ranch. Here they could live out their lifelong fantasy of being a real old-time cowboy. Each week Frank received letters from cowboys through the West looking for work. Word spread quickly that Frank's ranch used no trucks or tractors. He even received letters from several movie producers wanting to come out and look at the cowboys and the ranch, but Frank refused this. He would not become a geek for any man or any amount of money. The cowboys respected Frank. He could ride with the best of them and rope well enough. They liked the fact he was a man of few words, and looking at him when he looked at his ranch, they knew he loved his land.

After a few weeks a newly hired hand would be pulled into the cameraderie of the ranch. "I work on the Billings ranch," the cowboy would say with pride, meaning: I am a true cowboy. Frank wanted to hire a cook, but Mary would hear nothing of it. She rose in the morning and cooked for the men and at night when they came in tired and dirty their dinner was hot and ready. A good feeling surrounded the ranch. At times Frank alone on the ranch would feel the spirits of the Indians and the Mexicans around him, and he knew they were happy. Here was a man who stood up for what the land was. Here was a man who did not rape the land nor dig it with smoke-belching machines nor want to take anything from it. Frank would laugh looking at his cowboys, saying, hell, all we need is a train to rob somewhere. The cowboys to a man had several things in common. One, they all hated the government. They didn't like police and they hated a man who wanted to know everybody's business. The ranch was a sanctuary from the world, a place that would forever be the true West. A place a man born too late could live and dream about another day and another time.

Frank drove the truck slowly down the highway. He felt happy and elated. The cattle had all been rounded up for the winter and beef prices were up. What with paying little for gasoline and machinery, he had made a good profit. He had layed off four of the cowboys for the winter, but they would be back in the spring with a guaranteed job. For now they would go to Arizona and look for work during the winter. Two cowboys would stay to do the odds and ends that came up during the winter, which was mostly sitting by the pot-bellied stove in the bunkhouse and bullshitting the cold months by.

Frank turned the truck down the dirt road that led to the headquarters of the Buxley Ranch. He did not really know Buxley. It was strange, he thought, how one could live so close to man for years and not see him very often. Buxley was a big oil man from Texas who bought the ranch years earlier more for a write-off and to have parties at. When the phone rang and Buxley with his Texas drawl asked him to come to the party, Frank had not really wanted to go, but his mother told him, "Frank you should go, meet some people, have a good time."

Frank stopped the truck and looked at the Buxley house. It was not a house. It was a mansion. Built with its back up against a rock bluff it looked like a southern plantation home. Parked in the large oval driveway were Mercedes Benz automobiles, two Rolls Royces and numerous Cadillacs. South of the house was an airstrip and several shiny airplanes were tethered down. Frank stepped out of the truck. Walking towards the front door he brushed the front of his white cowboy shirt and looked at the crease in his Levis. He had bought a new white hat and a pair of boots for the party. A Mexican lady in a traditional maid's outfit answered his knock.

"Come in, sir," she said. Frank took off his hat and stepped into the room. Walking through a small hallway he gave his hat to a man and went into a room the size of his complete ranch house. There were over fifty people in the room, and in the corner a country band with blue pants and blue shirts and red kerchiefs around their necks played. A large, big-shouldered man walked up to him smiling an expansive, toothy grin.

"Frank," he spoke, extending his hand, "I'm glad you could make it." After shaking his hand, Mr. Buxley raised his glass and spoke above the noise of the crowd. "Friends, this here is Frank. This is the man I've been telling you about who owns the ranch across the way that is just like the old days, strictly a horse operation."

The faces of the crowd looked at Frank and it seemed to Frank they all smiled identically. Buxley still smiling looked at Frank, "Walk around, Frank, meet some new people. There's enough money in the room to buy New Mexico."

Frank took a scotch and water from a passing tray and stood observing the people. He had never seen so many diamonds on ladies, nor so many gold watches and gold belt buckles on men. Looking at the men's feet he guessed there was a small fortune in exotic leather boots. As Frank scanned the crowd he was thankful he was what he was. If I had all the money in the world, I wouldn't be like this, he told himself. Seeing an empty chair close to the band, Frank walked over and sat down. Frank noticed the many beautiful women, and for a moment he felt very empty. It was strange he knew, but he had only been on a few dates in his life. One to the senior prom, which turned out to be a big fiasco since he didn't know how to dance, and one when he was twenty-three. Jesus, he thought, I'm twenty-eight years old now, and I haven't slept with a woman.

But looking at the crowd, Frank could not help but look at the ladies and the way their blouses clung to their breasts, or how their hair moved when they talked. He did not notice the girl sit down in the chair next to him until he felt a light touch on his shoulder. Turning, his eyes met the eyes of the girl and it was as if invisible hands reached out and touched his heart. He felt a sudden flood of warmth spread across his shoulders. "Hi," she spoke with a slight Texas accent. Frank did not answer, stunned by the beauty of the lady. Her hair was auburn and fell down just touching the tops of her shoulders. Her eyes were dark brown and seemed to captivate his vision. He noticed the curve of her red lips and the way the small gold chain around her neck glistened as if it was a part of her skin. "Hi," she spoke again, a smile creasing her mouth.

Frank smiled back and blurted without thinking, "You're beautiful." No sooner were the words out of his mouth than he stammered, "I'm sorry, that was rude of me."

The lady reached and touched his hand with hers. "Telling a lady she is beautiful is nothing to be sorry about."

Leaning back in her chair, Frank saw the way her breasts strained against the thin silk of her blouse. Crossing her legs the skirt resting above her knee, he looked at the smooth lines of her calves. The lady smiled once again, "Like what you see?"

Frank sipped his drink. "Jesus, you knocked me off my feet."

The lady stood and took his hand, "Dance with me, cowboy."

"I can't dance," Frank answered.

"Who cares? I'll show you."

Standing with his arms around the lady, Frank was oblivious to the people around them. Only the girl's smile and perfume swam in front of his eyes. "All right," she spoke, "you move your left foot this way, then your right this way, and then take two quick little steps." Frank stumbled along but soon had a passable version of the Texas Two-Step. "All right," the lady taunted, "you're getting there."

Walking back to the chairs, the girl held onto Frank's arm and he could feel the soft swell of her breast against his upper arm. Sitting back down the girl took another drink from a passing tray and spoke, "So you're the man who runs a ranch like old-time cowboys."

Frank looked at her, "You sound like that's funny."

"No, no," she responded. "I just wonder why."

"What's your name?" Frank asked.

"My name is Sylvia Barnes. I am twenty-six years old and my father is an oil man. Is that enough information?"

Frank, feeling not so nervous, grinned, "That's enough."

"So tell me, why do you want to run a ranch the old-fashioned way? There couldn't be a lot of money in it."

Frank sipped his drink, "It's not for the money, it's for the land."

Sylvia nodded her head, "True die-hard cowboy you are, then — fight change, fight government, fight everything. Just give you the land and leave you alone and you can forget time."

Frank nodded his head, "I suppose that's true enough."

He noticed the gold bracelet around Sylvia's wrist as she sipped her drink and the large diamond earrings that shone from her ears when her hair moved. "So if I'm a die-hard cowboy, what are you?"

"Few words and right to the point, huh? Well, let me see, I went to a private high school and then attended a very good private school in Europe. Since then I have worked for my father. Doing nothing, really. He gives me a title to one of his companies and pays me for being his daughter. Beats working."

Frank stood and held out his hand, "Would you like to go outside and get some air?"

Sylvia took his hand, "I'd love to."

Outside they stood and watched as the sun slowly disappeared. "It's so peaceful out here," Sylvia murmured. "No hustle, no bustle of traffic, no great rush to be anywhere."

Frank looked at the lady as the sinking sun sent golden rays dancing across her form. She was the most beautiful woman he had ever seen in his life, and he knew looking at her that he was in love. He wanted to reach out and pull Sylvia into his arms. He wanted to run his hands through her hair and tell her how he needed her. It was absurd, it was insane, but it was true.

"What are you driving?" Sylvia asked.

"Not a Mercedes," Frank grinned. "I'm driving that pickup truck over there."

Sylvia started walking towards the truck and Frank watched the way her slender hips moved as she walked. "Take me for a ride, cowboy," she laughed.

"Where?" Frank blurted.

"Anywhere," her voice floated back.

They drove, Sylvia's form shadowed by the lights from the dash of the truck. "Miles and miles of nothing out here," she spoke, "so free, so untamed." Sylvia moved over and her side melted into Frank's side. "Ever make love to a stranger?" she teased, running her hands through the hair on the back of Frank's neck. Frank shook his head no, feeling a knot grow in his stomach. He wanted to tell her he had never made love to anybody in his life, but he could not. "Well, cowboy, how would you like to make love to me?"

Frank looked at Sylvia, "I'd like that very much."

"Do you have a blanket or anything?"

Frank always had a blanket in his truck. Driving miles to town and back you never knew when the truck would break down and it made for a much easier night with a blanket. Frank took a dirt road off the highway and drove for several miles. Stopping by a stand of cedar trees they got out. Sylvia spread the blanket out on the ground. Frank sat down. Sylvia looked up and into the thousands of stars and then looking at Frank sitting, she began to slowly unbutton her blouse. Her fingers moved delicately from button to button until peeling off her blouse, her breasts shone in the moonlight. She then took off her shoes and slowly wiggled out of her skirt. Then sitting down by Frank, she removed her stockings, her fingers lingering on her long flowing legs. As she took off her panties, she looked at Frank, "Come on, cowboy, let's see what you have to offer."

Standing, Frank removed his shirt and Sylvia ran her fingers over the muscles on his chest. With his pants and boots off they stood naked under the night. Frank held the girl and he had never felt the feelings that raced through his body. His heart pounded in his chest, his lips sought Sylvia's lips and they were like coals as they met. Sylvia's tongue darted across his lips and her hand swept down around his manhood. Frank ran his hands down her back and stroked the roundness of her fanny. His fingers moved up her side and to the richness of her breasts. Hungrily his lips sought her nipples and in one swift motion he lay her back on the blanket and entered her body. They did not move slowly but drove their bodies into each other like wild horses. Sylvia dug her nails into Frank's back and her moans and cries were like cries of beasts. Frank felt the wetness of the woman and the burning heat of her breath against his shoulder as their arms grew tighter and tighter around each other other and their bodies ached for release. With one final drive Frank emptied into the girl and a low deep moan emitted from his mouth. They lay quietly, Frank kissing her shoulder, keeping weight on his elbows as not to crush her against the ground. Slowly Sylvia ran her fingers along Frank's back at the same time running her tongue against his ear. Frank felt himself grow hard once again and he began to move his hips once more. Sylvia responded and once again they began to thrash like beasts.

"Harder, harder," Sylvia pleaded and Frank, caught in her spell, drove into her with all his might. And then with one large convulsion he came like a rushing river and Sylvia's cries split the night. "Frank, O Frank," she moaned, "you are the best, the best."

Riding back to the party, they were silent. Frank wanted to tell Sylvia he loved her. He wanted to take her home immediately and introduce her to his mother. He wanted to take her out and show her the ranch and tell her all about his life. Back at the party, they walked in smiling and talking, hand in hand. Several women sitting, looked at Sylvia, "Well, looks like she found her another cowboy to fuck," one snickered. "If she slept with 100 in the past year I wouldn't be surprised." Her friend looked at her, "Don't you wish you had, my dear?" Both women clinked their glasses together and looked for their husbands.

It was two in the morning when Frank left the party. He was drunk and happy. "I'll be here for a week," Sylvia told him, kissing his cheek, "Call me tomorrow and I'll come over to your ranch."

Driving back to the ranch Frank had never felt so happy. On his skin he could smell Sylvia's perfume. Her face swam in front of him and the taste of her breasts lingered on his lips. Back home and lying on his bed, he wanted to get up and drive back to the Buxley ranch and take Sylvia once more out to the trees.

The next afternoon Sylvia drove to the ranch. Frank, introducing her to his mother, was happier than he had ever been in his life. But Mary, shaking hands with the girl, felt a cold chill run up her spine and she had to force a smile. Watching Frank and Sylvia walk off, she wanted to run to her son and tell him this woman was no good, but she hid the feeling and went back into the house.

For a week Frank and Sylvia were together. They made love in the truck, in the hay barn and in a motel in Santa Fe. When Sylvia flew back to Dallas, driving back to the ranch Frank felt as though his heart had been torn from his body. Back at the ranch standing alone in the front yard he could not see the land around him or feel the fall breezes. There were no ghosts of Indians or Spaniards, no Mexicans looking for new life. No memories of his father or grandfather. There was only a void in his heart and a phone number etched in his mind.

That night sitting in his room, Frank took the spear point once more out of his drawer. Holding it in his hands, for the first time the point felt cold and lifeless, but as he turned it, faintly glowing

160

in the point's center, the image of the girl with the blonde hair appeared and spoke, "Frank, Frank, I love you."

Lying in bed Frank did not see the image of the blonde but only the whiteness of Sylvia's breast under the starlight as she removed her blouse.

CHAPTER 6
THE LAND STAYS

Frank sat on the rock wall that at one time had stretched across the mouth of the box canyon. His horse stood motionless, lazily swatting the flies that buzzed around his rump with his tail. It was a hot July day. A good day for sitting in the shade around the house and sipping iced tea. But for Frank it was just another gloomy day like the last nine months. Frank looked out upon the land, but it was as though the pinon and cedar that covered part of the ranch was nothing but a grey lifeless mass of nothingness. He did not feel the sweat drip down his forehead or hear the flies that buzzed by his ears. He was only conscious of the deep emptiness and pain that engulfed his heart and mind. Jesus Christ, he thought, how could things have gotten so bad?

Life was so good after he met Sylvia. She would call him at night or he would call her. They spent hours on the phone. Frank feeling as though he could reach out and touch his love. The sound of her voice coming like music over the miles. Each day working on the ranch was as though for the first time in his life he was in tune with the earth around him. There was love and life in all things. Before Sylvia he loved the land. But it was more a love out of sadness. He felt a kinship with the trees and earth of the ranch. He felt a bond with time on his land, but he had never felt love around him. But with Sylvia all life and creation on the ranch seemed to be an extension of Sylvia. With the love of Sylvia and running the ranch, Frank was happier than he had been in his complete life. It was as though he had been able to freeze time. Sitting around the fire at night out on the ranch with the other cowboys, the horses hobbled outside the glow of the fire, he and his men were beyond the grasp of the modern day world. There was no sound of the T.V. or radio telling of numerous disasters, no news of another war or the threat of the bomb or water pollution. On the ranch there was only the sound of the wind and the bellow of the cattle and the sound of horses and men working as one. Sylvia would love it, Frank had felt. Raised by a wealthy man, living her life from condo to condo. She would love the ranch and the feel of the seasons. She would ride with him out upon the land and he would show to her all the things he held dear in his life. They would search for arrowheads in the old ruin. They would have picnics out under the blue sky. For the first time in her life she would not be encumbered by buildings and automobiles. She would be free, able to see life for what it really was. A place, a moment in time, not a tall building or a nice car, not a deadline or an airline ticket to a new place.

They were married on the ranch. Brad flew in from California with his wife and children to be best man. Sylvia's father brought in a band and there were many people from Texas Frank did not know. The party after the wedding lasted until the early morning, but by midnight Sylvia and Frank slipped off and drove to town where they had a suite rented for the weekend. They loved passionately for two days and after the two days, Frank felt like a guilty child bringing Sylvia back to his mother and the ranch.

But within two weeks things started to change. Sylvia did not like to get up early and she made no effort to help Mary with any of the work. Mary was sixty-two years old now and needed help with breakfast for the cowboys. But Sylvia would only look at Frank and say quietly, "Hire a cook and a maid. I've never cooked or done housework in my life." At first Frank thought she was kidding and let it pass, but in time he knew she was not kidding and he would find himself looking at Sylvia and realizing she was a stranger to him. She would spend half the day doing her nails and hair and then the rest of the time sitting in front of the T.V. being bored. Every night she wished to go into town either to dance or eat out. But Frank after working all day was tired. He wanted to eat and rest or sit on the porch and talk.

After three months coming back to the ranch house one afternoon his mother was in the front yard with a worried look on her face. As he approached she spoke, "She's gone." "Who's gone?" Frank asked. "Sylvia. She left you this," and Mary handed Frank a sealed envelope. Sitting down on a bench beneath a cottonwood tree, Frank ripped the envelope open, and read: Frank, I am going home to my father. There is nothing here for me. You will hear from my attorney. And it was signed simply, Sylvia. Frank let the letter fall to the ground and he exhaled loudly. Around him all was darkness and it was as though he was sitting in a void alone and cold.

Mary did not go to him during the evening as he sat silently. There was nothing she could say or do, only know in her heart her initial feeling about Sylvia had been true. She was a cold, self-centered woman who had only wanted her son for what she could get out of him.

A week later Frank received a letter certified mail from Harlington and Jones Attorneys at Law from Dallas. Sylvia was filing for divorce under mental cruelty and since New Mexico was a community property state, Frank would owe Sylvia half of everything he owned. Because of slick legal work on paper, Sylvia owned nothing. The letter went on that at current land prices the way they were, Frank owed Sylvia close to $400,000. Frank was devastated. There was no way he could raise that kind of money. If he could borrow it on the ranch it would not take the banks long to foreclose on his land and he would have nothing. Within another month the divorce was final and Frank had been given a court order giving him one year to hand over the settlement of $390,000 or half of the ranch.

Sitting in the living room Frank felt a deep encompassing desolation settle over him. He should have known, he told himself, the signs were always there before his eyes. Sylvia's clothes were not the clothes of a ranch lady, her smile was too quick, her body too lush to ever have a feeling of the land. But even in his pain he could not force himself to hate Sylvia. For the brief months he felt feelings he never knew existed in his body or mind. Lying with her after making love there was deep peace and contentment that settled over him. Far deeper than he ever felt with the land or anybody else in his life.

A large dust devil swept by close to Frank, spraying him with fine dust and moving him from his thoughts. He stood up from the rock wall and looked back into the mouth of the box canyon. Not far from where he was standing he had seen the mutilated body of the Indian the winter day with his father. Standing engrossed in his despair, Frank heard the wails of women come floating out of the canyon and there before him were many Indians. On the steep walls of the canyon braves sat, bows in hand, and further into the canyon women and children huddled in makeshift shelters. Turning away from the canyon he saw over a hundred warriors dressed for battle waiting to attack the canyon. Turning once again he saw a slender Indian girl who did not cry with the other women but stood, her eyes lost in deep grief. And for a brief moment he was inside the vision and a sadness deeper than his swept through his body that made him fall to his knees. Falling, the images left and Frank blinked his eyes, rising, and remounting his horse headed for the ranch house. The ride had done him no good, there were still no answers to his problem. He would have to deed over half of the ranch. After all the years, he would give up land that had been in his family for over a century. Riding, Frank could see his grandfather when he was a young man on the land, and he could see his grandfather's father piling the rocks at the corners of the ranch and proclaiming to the world this was his land and letting all men know he would die for what was his. He could see his father working his life away on the land and he could see himself an old man walking across the face of the ranch. Unsaddling the horse in the barn, Frank put the saddle on the saddle rack and spoke to himself, "I have failed. I have failed in my responsibility to my family."

Although the cowboys working the ranch knew something was wrong with Frank, they did not know the extent of the consequences of his divorce. Many of the men had been married and divorced. It was part of being a cowboy. But being poor, they did not understand settlements. Life for them did not change. They rode the range. Fixed the fences. Doctored the sick cows and branded the young. But they did miss Frank. He no longer went out with the cowboys but stayed away, spending his days riding on the ranch or doing small tasks around the headquarters. He'll get over it, one would say, life goes on. It takes time, another would add his advice.

Mary could not reach her son. She had tried many times. "It will be okay, Frank, give her half of the property. We'll make it, It's not right, I know, but it is how it is." Frank would only look at her and shake his head, trying not to believe the facts. There was something, somewhere there was an answer. He just did not know it yet.

Several land developers from town hearing about his plight had called him and offered him money for parts of the ranch. "We'll divide the property and sell ten to fifty acre parcels and call them ranchettes." Frank solemnly told them no. He would not have pseudo cowboys from L.A. and Chicago running around on his property. They could buy their remnants of the West someplace else. As long as it was possible the ranch would be as it was now. A true part of the American West. A ranch owned by a man whose entire family had been ranchers.

Frank sat in his room and for the first time in months he thought about the spear point. Taking it from his drawer, the point seemed lusterless, the black dull like coal, and it lay cold and lifeless in his hand. Lying down on his bed, Frank looked deep into the point, but there was nothing. "The magic is gone," he murmured to himself, and as he was about to set the point down on the nightstand, a face of a girl with blonde hair appeared from within the point. "Frank," the face spoke, "I love you, I love you.' Frank, seeing the image, did not smile but turned off the light and tried to sleep.

But sleep did not come. He lay, his mind racked by dreams that did not correlate. And in the morning when he rose with the sun, he felt tired and depressed.

Standing outside the house Frank looked out past the alfalfa field his father had started and across to the horse corrals and the outbuildings, and he relized that he would be the last of the line to own this property. Without a son to carry on the ranch, then the ranch would surely die. He also knew that the half he would have to give to Sylvia would be subdivided and split into small parcels and sold to the people he most disliked. And with this he no longer felt grief for himself but for the land around him. And he thought after all the time and years the land would finally succumb. Going back inside the house Frank took the spear point from his drawer and put it in his back pocket. He took his Colt 357 pistol from the closet. His mother was in the kitchen cooking, but Frank said nothing to her as he left. In the barn he saddled a horse and rode off into the interior of the ranch.

With the holster and pistol strapped to his leg, riding Frank once again felt like an old-time cowboy. He had tried his best to make the ranch work, returnng it to the old ways, and it had worked but because of his heart, he had lost the land. Frank looked out upon the ranch and he could see the land before there were fences, cutting across the face of the ranch. He could see Indians moving over the earth not concerned with titles and deeds but in tune with the land. He could see Spaniards looking at the land as a possession, a thing to add to their list of glory and power. And he could see the poor Mexican families coming to the land looking for hope and a future. He could feel his relatives upon the land, making the land a part of their heart and soul. Lost in his thoughts, he remembered his young years when he went out upon the land silent and searching, watching the ghosts and spirits as they told him of their past lives. The ghosts seeking a man who would know and understand what the land had been to them. Seeking a man who did not want the land to become ranchettes and homesites. Seeking a man who would let the land live and be only what it was, the land. With these thoughts Frank began to feel there was no place in the world for him. What was he but some dumb cowboy? All he knew was this land, this parcel of land that to the rest of the world was but a commodity. He could not go into town and be a banker or a doctor or a lawyer. He couldn't run a store or work in a gas station, and he felt without the land there was no reason for his life. It was true what his mother had always told him, he was a part of the land, the land was his true mother.

Frank rode slowly looking out upon the ranch. He rode until he came to the edge of the sandy clay-based slope that ran down from the mesa top to the Mexican homesteader's rock home and the Indian ruins. Dismounting from his horse he did not look at the ruins or the Mexican shack but gazed at the old church. And looking at the old church he wished that he could pray, but no words came to his mind. Sitting down, Frank watched and a short pudgy priest walked out of the church. In the vision the church was not old, it was new. The mud walls still damp and the priest was smiling. The priest walked slowly around his church, touching the walls and looking into the heavens. Turning his gaze to the Mexican shack, Frank saw a man and a woman walking hand in hand towards the small river that ran behind the church. Drawing close to the church, the woman reached out and took the hand of the priest and the three stood smiling at each other. Then from the Indian ruin children began to run towards the three people. Hand in hand they formed a circle around the adults and they started skipping around the priest and the Mexican couple. Then from the pueblo an old blind man, led by a lame woman, walked out and stretched his hands towards the sky and Frank could hear the man say, "Bless us, mother earth, you who have forsaken us." Turning his gaze from the images, Frank saw riding across the mesa top a lone Indian brave, hanging from his waist by a cord was the black spear point. Frank could see the pain and anguish on the brave's face as he stopped his horse and looked down at the pueblo. Frank blinked his eyes and rubbed his face. Standing he looked off towards the horizon, towards a stand of cottonwood trees. Here he could see a small dust cloud that marked the advancing column of Spanish soldiers as they left the garrison. And then all the images came together as if they were pulled into each other by a magnet and after they were pulled together there was nothing but the land and the ruins and the low moan of wind sweeping over the earth.

Frank sat back down on the edge of the slope. Inside himself there were no feelings. Reaching into his pocket, Frank took out the black obsidian spear point. It lay in his hand as cold as ice. Digging with his other hand, Frank dug a hole in the ground beside where he sat and lay the point in the hole. Looking at the point at the bottom of the hole one last time, he pushed the earth over the point and mumbled, "You belong with the earth, your destiny is not finished, your magic is no longer for me."

Frank reached to his leg and removed the pistol from its holster. Holding the pistol his eyes scanned the land around him. There were no ghosts or images transcending time. There were only the lifeless ruins with their crumbling walls and rocks telling of death and lost dreams. There was Devil's Peak with the pictographs of men who had succumbed to their own mortality. And the ageless pinon and cedar trees that were oblivious to all around them. Overhead two hawks circled and watched the land below, not interested in the lone figure on the edge of the slope. Frank took a deep breath and raised the pistol and set the barrel against his temple. Holding the pistol to his head, peace settled over him. Soon I will be a ghost, he thought, soon I will be one of the images. Forever part of this land.

He slowly pulled the hammer back on the pistol and took a deep breath. Beside him the horse stood motionless, its large brown eyes staring into oblivion. As his finger tightened on the trigger, Frank's eyes roamed down the slope towards the ruins and he smiled to himself. But then his finger froze, and he stopped, the gun still pointed at his head as his eyes focused on something he had never seen before.

At the base of the slope a strange object protruded from the clay-based soil. Frank felt confused. He had been in this spot hundreds of times in his life and had never seen this before. Slowly he lowered his hand and rested the pistol on the ground. He stood and looked more closely at the object. It looked like a horse's hoof. Frank stepped over the side of the slope and scrambled down the cliff. Standing beside the protruding bone he saw the old iron shoe nailed to the ancient hoof. Digging with his hands, he uncovered a horse and the remnants of a saddle. Lower, below the horse, was a rifle rusted past recognition, but here also was the skeleton of a man and two silver spurs as good as if they had been placed here yesterday.

Digging on, Frank found more bones and then as he dug faster with his hands, he found the first bar of gold. Picking up the heavy bar, crusted with dirt, he took out his pocketknife and scraped the surace. The bright yellow shone through time like the sun. Frank let out a yell and dug furiously. Within an hour with the sweat streaming down his face, Frank had a pile which consisted of 30 bars of gold. Frank estimated the gold bars at being close to twenty pounds each. Six hundred pounds of gold at the current market was close to $400,000. Frank scrambled up the face of the slope and picked up his pistol. He mounted his horse and galloped back to the ranch headquarters, thinking about his grandfather's story of the bandit when he was very young. And he rememberd the vision of the man on the ridge with his three mules and knew this was the bandit. At the house he jumped in the truck and drove back out to the ruin and put the gold in the truck. Returning to the ranch he ran into the house where his mother was in the kitchen. He hugged her tightly, "Look, come look!" he spoke excitedly. Standing by the truck, looking at the gold, Mary began to cry. It was a miracle. Frank went inside the house and dialed Sylvia's number in Dallas. When she answered, Frank spoke plainly: "The land stays," and hung up.

Frank went back outside and remounted his horse. He rode swiftly back to the spot above the slope. Searching the ground he looked for the fresh dirt where he had buried the spear point. Finding it, he dug up the point and held it in his hands. Standing he held the point up to the sky and the deep black luster once again came alive in his hand. He could see the Indians and the Mexicans and the small priest within the point, and then before him came the vision of the girl. The blonde lady, her hair falling around her face. and Frank could see the smooth glow of her face and the red outline of her lips as she spoke, "Frank, Frank, I love you." Frank put the point back into his pocket and remounted his horse. Riding back to the ranch headquarters, he saw the deep colors of the earth around him and knew that once agin, the land was his. Once again he would fight time with a ranch that used only horses and cowboys and once again the visions were his. And sitting on his horse, surrounded by he land and the sky and the circling hawks, Frank knew he would love, somewhere, someplace, was a blonde-haired woman with kind gentle eyes who waited for his touch.

That night, lying in bed as sleep was about to blanket him, Frank saw a Mexican riding a horse and behind him were three mules loaded down with heavy packs. The Mexican rode, spurring his horse on, and as he rode his eyes turned and bore into Frank's eyes and the image spoke, "I have not died in vain. I have not died in vain." Frank closed his eyes, the image of the bandit slowly fading away as sleep overcame him.

Outside the wind blew gently. It came from the east, rising up and over the Ortiz gold mine and settled down into the valley below, caressing the pictographs on Devil's Peak. It gained speed and swept over the ruins of the church and Mexican homesteader's shack. It kicked the dust from around the Indian ruin and then turned and circled the Ortiz hacienda. As Frank slept it touched gently on his window and then was gone with the night like a dream.